THE TWISTY SECRET OF SECRETS

A Thought-Provoking Novel

Scott F. McFarlin

ISBN: 978-1-257-85290-1

Published by: Sharp Press

TABLE OF CONTENTS

PREFACE: THE ASHFORD DISCOVERY

James Ashford - October 2024

Found among the papers of my late grandmother's estate were documents I was never meant to see. Hidden behind a false wall in our family's Connecticut home, these records tell a story that spans seven centuries—a story of sacrifice, secrecy, and an impossible choice that has shaped our world in ways no history book will ever record.

What follows are the authentic accounts of six bloodlines bound by an ancient covenant. Each generation believed they understood their purpose. Each was only partially right.

I publish these now because the time for secrets has ended. The world has changed, the old agreements are breaking down, and humanity deserves to know the truth about those who walk among us—and the price they have paid to keep us all safe.

The names have not been changed. These people lived. Their choices matter. Their story continues.

—James Ashford, Historian October 13, 2025.

CHAPTER 1: THE VISION OF ENDING

The fever had taken hold of her mother three days ago, and Eleanor Blackthorne knew—with that peculiar certainty that had plagued her since childhood—that by sunset, she would be alone in the world.

She pressed the damp cloth to her mother's burning forehead, watching the labored rise and fall of her chest. The black swellings beneath Margaret Blackthorne's arms had grown larger overnight, dark and terrible against her pale skin. Eleanor had seen enough of these symptoms in recent months to know their meaning, but this knowing felt different somehow. Deeper. As if the knowledge came not from observation but from some place inside her that saw beyond the present moment.

"Eleanor, child." Her mother's voice was barely a whisper. "Where is your father?"

"Still in the village, tending to the Millers' boy." Eleanor dipped the cloth in cool water again. "He'll be back soon."

Margaret's eyes, still bright with fever, focused on her daughter's face. "You know, don't you? You always know."

Eleanor's hand stilled. "Know what, Mother?"

"When someone is..." Margaret's breath caught. "You've always had that way about you. Even as a babe, you'd cry when the old ones were near their time. Your father thought it was just coincidence, but I knew better."

The admission hung in the air like incense. Eleanor had never spoken of the feelings that came to her—the inexplicable certainty about who would live through the night and who wouldn't, the way she could sense sickness in people before they showed symptoms, the dreams that sometimes came true in disturbing detail. In a world where such knowledge could brand a person as cursed, or worse, she had learned to keep her knowing to herself.

"Rest now," Eleanor said, avoiding her mother's piercing gaze. "Save your strength."

But Margaret's hand found hers, surprisingly strong for someone so near death. "Promise me something, child. Whatever gift God has given you, use it wisely. The world has little patience for those who see too clearly."

Before Eleanor could respond, her mother's grip loosened, and she slipped back into fevered sleep.

Eleanor sat back in the wooden chair that had been her post for three days, studying her mother's face in the golden morning light filtering through their cottage's single window. The knowing pressed against her consciousness like a physical weight. Not just about her mother—that certainty had settled in her chest days ago—but about something else. Something vast and terrible approaching like a storm on a clear day.

The door creaked open, and her father entered, his shoulders stooped with exhaustion. Thomas Blackthorne had aged a decade in the past months as the Great Mortality swept through their village of Ravenscroft. Once the most sought-after healer in three counties, he now moved like a man haunted by his own helplessness.

"How is she?" he asked, though Eleanor could tell by his expression that he already knew the answer.

"The same." Eleanor stood and moved to the hearth, where a pot of weak barley soup simmered. "You should eat something."

"In a moment." Thomas knelt beside his wife's bed, taking her hand in both of his. "The Miller boy?"

"Dead before I arrived." Thomas's voice carried no emotion anymore. After watching so many fail despite his efforts, he had learned to protect himself by feeling nothing at all. "They're preparing the pyre now."

Eleanor ladled soup into a wooden bowl and set it on the table. "Father, there's something I need to tell you."

"What is it, child?"

The words died in her throat. How could she explain the certainty that grew stronger each day? That this plague was only the beginning? That something worse was coming—not a disease of the body, but a sickness of the spirit that would consume the world itself?

Instead, she said, "The Hartwells' baby—she's going to be fine. The fever will break tonight."

Thomas looked up from his wife's bedside, studying Eleanor's face. "How can you know that?"

"The same way I know Mother won't see another sunrise."

The words escaped before she could stop them, and she immediately regretted their bluntness. But Thomas only nodded slowly, as if he had been waiting for this conversation for years.

"Your mother thinks it's a gift from God," he said quietly. "I've always worried it might be something else entirely."

"What do you mean?"

"In my travels, before you were born, I met others who claimed such abilities. Healers who could cure with a touch, seers who could read the future in flames, women who could call rain from clear skies." Thomas's voice dropped to barely above a whisper. "Most were burned as witches. The rest simply... disappeared."

Eleanor felt the blood drain from her face. "Are you saying I'm—"

"I'm saying you need to be careful, daughter. These are dangerous times for anyone who stands apart from the common folk."

Before Eleanor could respond, a commotion erupted outside their cottage. Voices shouting, the clatter of cart wheels, dogs barking in alarm. Thomas rose and moved to the window, cursing under his breath.

"What is it?" Eleanor asked.

"Refugees from Westhollow. Looks like half the village."

Eleanor joined him at the window and saw a ragged procession of perhaps twenty people making their way toward Ravenscroft's center. Men, women, and children, their faces hollow with hunger and terror, their belongings loaded onto a single cart pulled by an exhausted ox.

"I should go help them," Thomas said, already reaching for his leather satchel of healing supplies.

"Wait." Eleanor caught his arm, that familiar knowing washing over her like a tide. But this time, it was different. Stronger. More urgent. "Father, don't go. Not yet."

"Eleanor, these people need—"

"Something's wrong." The certainty built in her chest, pressing against her ribs like caged birds. "Something's coming with them. Something terrible."

Thomas studied her face for a long moment, then set down his satchel. "Tell me."

Eleanor closed her eyes, trying to make sense of the chaos of images and sensations flooding her mind. "There's a man among them. Tall, dark hair, wearing a monk's robe. He's... he's not what he seems."

"What do you mean?"

"I don't know." Frustration crept into her voice. "I just know that if you touch him, something will happen. Something that will change everything."

The sound of footsteps on the path outside their cottage interrupted her warning. Thomas moved to the door, but Eleanor grabbed his sleeve.

"Promise me," she said, echoing her mother's earlier words. "Promise you won't touch the monk. No matter what happens, don't let skin meet skin."

Thomas nodded slowly, though she could see the skepticism in his eyes. He opened the door to find a young woman standing on their threshold, her clothes torn and dirty, a baby clutched to her chest.

"Please," the woman gasped. "My child is burning with fever. They said Thomas Blackthorne lived here, that he could help."

Eleanor stepped forward, studying the baby's flushed face. The knowing whispered its familiar certainty: the child would live, but barely. She would carry scars from this fever for the rest of her life, marks that would mark her as different.

"Bring her in," Thomas said, stepping aside.

The woman entered gratefully, followed by several other refugees. Eleanor watched from the corner as her father examined the baby, his practiced hands gentle and sure. But her attention was drawn to the figure standing in their doorway—a tall man in a brown monk's robe, his hood pulled up despite the warmth of the morning.

"Brother Augustine," the woman said, noticing Eleanor's stare. "He's been traveling with us since Westhollow fell. A holy man."

The monk stepped forward, and Eleanor felt every instinct in her body scream in warning. There was something about him that made her skin crawl, something that had nothing to do with his appearance and everything to do with the wrongness that seemed to emanate from his very being.

"God's blessing on this house," the monk said, his voice cultured and smooth. "I wonder if I might impose upon your hospitality for a cup of water? The road has been long and difficult."

Thomas looked up from his examination of the baby. "Of course, Brother. Eleanor, would you—"

"I'll get it," Eleanor said quickly, moving toward the water barrel in the corner of the room. Anything to keep her father away from the monk.

But as she filled a wooden cup, the monk moved closer to where Thomas knelt with the baby. Eleanor watched in growing alarm as the man extended his hand, ostensibly to bless the child, but she could see the deliberate way he positioned himself so that any movement from her father would result in contact.

"Father," she called, trying to keep her voice calm. "The baby needs—"

Her words were lost as Thomas shifted position, his hand brushing against the monk's outstretched fingers for the briefest instant.

The world exploded.

Eleanor felt the cup slip from her grasp as reality fractured around her. Time stretched and compressed, colors bled together, and sound became a roar that seemed to come from inside her own skull. But this wasn't happening to her—it was happening to the monk, whose calm facade had shattered the moment he touched her father.

Through the chaos, she saw him clearly for the first time. Not a holy man at all, but something else. Something that could see beyond the present moment, just as she could, but with a power that dwarfed her own small gift.

And in that moment of contact, his visions became hers.

The world spun away from the cottage, away from England, away from the year 1348 entirely. Eleanor found herself standing in a place that existed outside of time, watching the future unfold like scenes from a fever dream.

She saw people—her descendants, perhaps, or the descendants of others like the monk—who could do things that defied all natural law. A woman who could heal any wound with a touch of her hand. A man who could move objects with his mind, lifting stones as large as houses without effort. Children who could become invisible at will, who could speak to animals, who could command fire and water and wind itself.

At first, the visions were wondrous. She saw these gifted ones using their abilities to help humanity—ending famines, stopping plagues, preventing wars through the sheer impossibility of their gifts. The world became a paradise where suffering was a choice rather than an inevitability.

But then the vision darkened.

Fear crept into the hearts of ordinary people as they realized the extent of these abilities. Governments began to hunt the gifted, capturing them for experimentation, trying to unlock their secrets or simply contain their power. Wars erupted—not between nations, but between the gifted and the ungifted, between those who would use their abilities openly and those who sought to hide.

Eleanor watched in horror as the paradise crumbled. The gifted, pressed by persecution and desperate to survive, began to use their powers not to help but to dominate. Cities burned under supernatural fire. Minds were enslaved by those who could control thoughts. The very elements turned against humanity as the gifted reshaped the world in their anger.

But the worst was yet to come.

As the conflict raged, something fundamental broke in the relationship between humanity and the earth itself. The constant use of supernatural power, the bending of natural law to human will, began to tear at the fabric of reality. Crops withered not from disease but from the simple wrongness that had infected the soil. Animals fled to the deepest wilderness, their instincts screaming that civilization had become anathema to life itself.

And in the end, Eleanor saw the last human settlement—a tiny cluster of buildings huddled against a landscape that looked like the surface of an alien world. Empty. Silent. Abandoned not to plague or war, but to the simple fact that the earth could no longer sustain the species that had learned to transcend its own nature.

A voice spoke from the darkness, and Eleanor realized it was her own: "When the gifts of the blood are known to all, the world shall choose fear over wonder, and in that choosing, find its ending."

The vision shattered like glass, and Eleanor found herself back in her family's cottage, lying on the floor with her father kneeling beside her, his face pale with concern. The refugees were gone— fled, apparently, when she had collapsed screaming. Only the monk remained, standing in the doorway with an expression of profound sadness.

"You saw it too," he said. It wasn't a question.

Eleanor struggled to sit up, her head spinning. "What... what was that?"

"The future. One possible future, among many." The monk lowered his hood, revealing a face much younger than his voice suggested, marked by eyes that held too much knowledge. "My name is Augustine, though I am no monk. I have been searching for others like us, those who can see beyond the present moment."

"Others like us?"

"Gifted with abilities that should not exist. Cursed with knowledge that should not be possessed." Augustine stepped fully into the cottage and closed the door behind him. "The vision you experienced—it was not just a possibility, but a certainty. Unless we act."

Thomas looked between them, his healer's mind struggling to make sense of what he had witnessed. "Eleanor, what is he talking about?"

Eleanor met her father's eyes, seeing her own fear reflected there. "The knowing I've always had—it's not just intuition, is it? It's something more."

"Much more," Augustine confirmed. "And you are not alone. Across England, across all of Europe, there are others awakening to abilities that should not exist. A healer whose touch can cure any ailment. A woman who can become one with shadows. A man whose very presence calms the most savage beast. They are beginning to discover their gifts, just as you have discovered yours."

"And if they do?" Eleanor asked, though she already knew the answer.

"Then the vision becomes reality. The world burns, humanity destroys itself, and the earth itself rejects our species as a failed experiment." Augustine moved closer, his expression urgent. "But there is another way."

Eleanor's mother stirred on her bed, her fever-bright eyes focusing on the three figures standing in her cottage. "Eleanor," she whispered. "What have you seen?"

Eleanor knelt beside her mother's bed, taking her burning hand. "The end of everything, Mother. The end of everything, unless we can find a way to prevent it."

Margaret's grip tightened with surprising strength. "Then prevent it, child. Whatever the cost, prevent it."

As if summoned by her words, a new certainty settled in Eleanor's chest. Not the knowing of death or disease, but something larger. A purpose that would consume the rest of her life and the lives of her descendants after her.

"How?" she asked Augustine. "How do we stop something that hasn't happened yet?"

"By making sure it never can happen," he replied. "By finding the others before they discover their gifts, and convincing them to hide what they are. By creating a covenant that will bind our bloodlines for generations—a promise that our abilities will remain secret, no matter the cost."

Eleanor looked around the cottage that had been her entire world— her dying mother, her exhausted father, the simple life that the vision had shown her was about to end forever. She thought of the paradise that could be, if only the gifted could use their abilities openly. But she also remembered the horror that paradise became, the empty settlement at the end of all things.

"And if we refuse? If we try to use our gifts to help people, as they're meant to be used?"

Augustine's expression grew infinitely sad. "Then your vision becomes prophecy, and the world ends within a generation."

Outside, the church bell began to toll—not the hourly chime, but the slow, steady rhythm that meant another soul had departed this life. Eleanor's knowing whispered that it was the Miller boy they had failed to save, and that by nightfall, three more would follow. Tomorrow, perhaps a dozen. The plague would take its course regardless of what supernatural gifts existed in the world.

19

But if those gifts became known...

"Mother," Eleanor said, turning back to the bed. But Margaret Blackthorne's eyes had already closed for the final time, her hand growing cool in Eleanor's grasp.

The knowing had been right, as it always was. By sunset, Eleanor would be alone in the world.

Except she wasn't alone, was she? Augustine was here, claiming there were others like them scattered across the continent. Others who would have to make the same impossible choice: help humanity and risk destroying it, or hide their gifts and watch the world suffer in ignorance.

Eleanor closed her mother's eyes gently, then stood and faced Augustine. "This covenant you speak of—what would it require?"

"Everything," he said simply. "The gifted must never reveal themselves, never use their abilities openly, never allow the world to know what we are capable of. We must live as shadows, helping when we can without being seen, guiding without being known."

"And our children? Our descendants?"

"They must be taught the same. Each generation must understand the price of revelation, must choose secrecy over recognition, must sacrifice their own authenticity for the survival of the species."

Eleanor thought of the vision again—not just the ending, but the paradise that came before it. Healers who could end suffering, seers who could prevent disasters, those who could reshape the very world to be kinder, more just, more beautiful.

All of it forbidden. All of it sacrificed to prevent a future that might never come to pass.

"How can we be certain?" she asked. "How can we know that hiding is the right choice?"

Augustine was quiet for a long moment. When he spoke, his voice carried the weight of terrible certainty. "Because I have seen not just one future, but many. In every timeline where the gifted reveal themselves, the world ends. In every possible future where our abilities become known, humanity chooses fear over wonder, and in that choosing, finds its destruction."

Eleanor nodded slowly, feeling the weight of destiny settle on her shoulders like a cloak she would never be able to remove. "Then we hide. We find the others, and we convince them to hide as well."

"It will not be easy," Augustine warned. "Many will resist. They will see their gifts as blessings meant to be shared, as responsibilities to help those who suffer. They will not understand that sometimes the greatest mercy is to do nothing."

"Then we make them understand." Eleanor moved to the window, looking out at the village where the plague still raged, where people died in agony while she possessed knowledge that could ease their passing. "Whatever it takes, we make them understand."

She turned back to Augustine, and for the first time since the vision, felt something like peace. Not happiness—she doubted she would ever feel truly happy again—but the calm that came with purpose.

"When do we begin?"

Augustine smiled, and for a moment he looked less like a bearer of terrible prophecies and more like a young man grateful not to bear his burden alone. "Now, if you're willing. There are others to find, and the future will not wait for our convenience."

Eleanor looked one last time at her mother's still form, then at her father, who had remained silent throughout their conversation but whose eyes held a mixture of grief and understanding.

"Go," Thomas said quietly. "Your mother was right—you have a gift, and the world needs you to use it wisely. Even if that means hiding it."

Eleanor kissed her father's forehead, knowing with that familiar certainty that she would never see him again. Then she gathered her few possessions and followed Augustine out into a world that would never know how close it had come to paradise, or how much had been sacrificed to keep it from destruction.

Behind them, the plague continued its relentless course, taking the lives that neither supernatural gift nor hidden knowledge could save. But ahead lay a different kind of future—one where the gifted would walk among humanity unseen, protecting the world from the very abilities that could transform it.

The covenant had begun.

CHAPTER 2: THE CALLING

The road to Dover stretched before them like a ribbon of dried mud and broken dreams. Eleanor walked beside Augustine's horse, her few possessions tied in a bundle across her shoulder, watching the countryside roll past in waves of abandonment. Empty farmsteads dotted the landscape, their doors hanging open like mouths frozen in eternal screams. The Great Mortality had swept through this region months ago, leaving behind a silence so complete it seemed to press against her eardrums.

Three days had passed since she left Ravenscroft, and already her father's cottage felt like something from another lifetime. The knowing that had always whispered at the edges of her consciousness now roared like a river in flood, bringing with it information she had never sought and understanding she wished she could unknow.

"Tell me about the touch," Augustine said, breaking the morning quiet. He had been patient with her grief, allowing her to process the magnitude of what lay ahead, but now his voice carried the urgency of their mission. "In your vision, you experienced my sight. But there was something more, wasn't there?"

Eleanor nodded, though she hadn't spoken of it yet. "When the stranger touched my hand—the man who died outside our cottage— something passed between us. Not just the vision, but something else. I could feel his memories, his last thoughts." She paused, studying a dead sparrow on the roadside. "I think I might be able to do it deliberately."

"Show me."

Augustine dismounted and extended his hand. Eleanor hesitated, remembering the overwhelming chaos of that first contact, but the certainty in her chest told her this was necessary. She reached out and grasped his fingers.

The world shifted.

Unlike the violent torrent of the first vision, this contact brought with it a controlled flow of images and sensations. She saw Augustine's memories: a monastery in Francia where he had first discovered his gift, the terror in the abbot's eyes when Augustine had described a vision of the monastery burning, the flight into exile when that very vision came to pass three days later. She felt his loneliness, the weight of carrying knowledge that no one else could understand, the desperate hope that had driven him to search for others like himself.

But beneath those surface memories lay something deeper—a network of connections, like golden threads stretching across the continent. Through Augustine's sight, she could sense them: other points of light scattered across Europe, each one a person carrying abilities that defied natural law.

Eleanor released his hand and staggered backward, her head spinning with the influx of information.

"You saw them," Augustine said. It wasn't a question.

"Dozens of them. Maybe hundreds." Eleanor pressed her palms against her temples, trying to organize the chaotic impressions. "There's a healer in Dover—a man named Thomas. His touch can draw sickness from a person's body and take it into himself. He's been working among the plague victims, saving lives, but..."

"But each healing leaves him weaker," Augustine finished. "Yes, I've sensed him as well. He's the reason we're traveling this direction."

"He's going to expose himself, isn't he?" Eleanor's knowing whispered the answer even as she asked the question. "He's going to try to heal too many at once, and people will realize his abilities aren't natural."

"Within a fortnight, if we don't reach him first."

They resumed walking, but Eleanor's mind remained focused on the network she had glimpsed through Augustine's perception. So many points of light, so many people struggling with abilities they didn't understand. In her vision, she had seen what would happen if those abilities became known to the world at large, but what about the individuals themselves? What happened to a healer who couldn't stop healing, even as it killed him? What became of someone who could read thoughts but couldn't stop the constant intrusion of other minds?

"Augustine," she said carefully, "how many of the gifted do you think survive long enough to master their abilities?"

His silence was answer enough.

They reached Dover as the sun began its descent toward the western horizon, painting the harbor in shades of gold and blood. The port city should have been bustling with merchants and fishermen, but the plague had taken its toll here as well. Ships sat abandoned at their moorings, their sails furled and their crews long dead or fled. The few people Eleanor saw moved with the careful haste of survivors who knew that lingering in any place too long invited disaster.

Augustine led them through the winding streets toward the poorest quarter of the city, where the sick had been left to die in hovels that decent folk avoided. The stench of death and human waste grew stronger with each step, until Eleanor had to breathe through her mouth to keep from retching.

"There," Augustine said, pointing to a low building that had once been a warehouse. "Can you feel him?"

Eleanor closed her eyes and extended her newfound sensitivity. The golden thread she had glimpsed in Augustine's memories was stronger here, pulsing with exhaustion and something that felt like desperation. "He's inside. But he's..." She opened her eyes, alarmed. "He's dying."

They hurried to the warehouse entrance, where a young woman sat guard with a rusty knife. Her clothes marked her as a prostitute, but her eyes held the fierce protectiveness of someone who had found something worth defending.

"You can't enter," she said, though her voice shook with fatigue. "Thomas is working. He can't be disturbed."

"We're here to help him," Eleanor said, and something in her tone must have convinced the woman, because she stepped aside without further argument.

The interior of the warehouse had been converted into a makeshift hospital. Dozens of plague victims lay on straw pallets, their bodies twisted with fever and pain. The sweet-sick smell of death competed with the sharper odor of herbs and poultices. And moving among them, barely able to stay upright, was the man Eleanor had seen in her vision-touch with Augustine.

Thomas was perhaps thirty years old, though suffering had aged him beyond his years. His dark hair was streaked with premature gray, and his skin had the translucent quality of someone who had pushed his body far beyond its natural limits. As Eleanor watched, he knelt beside a child whose breath came in shallow gasps. Thomas placed his hands on the boy's chest, and Eleanor felt the flow of power between them—the sickness leaving the child and entering the healer.

The boy's breathing eased, his fever broke, and he opened clear eyes for the first time in days. But Thomas collapsed forward, catching himself on his hands as blood dripped from his nose onto the straw.

"Enough," Eleanor said, crossing the warehouse floor in quick strides. "You're killing yourself."

Thomas looked up at her with eyes that held too much pain and too little hope. "One more," he whispered. "Just one more, and then I'll rest."

"No." Eleanor knelt beside him, feeling the weight of exhaustion that clung to him like a physical presence. "If you heal one more person in your condition, you'll die. And then who will help the others?"

"Better I die saving lives than live watching them suffer." Thomas tried to stand, but his legs wouldn't support him. "Who are you to tell me to stop?"

Eleanor looked around the warehouse, at the dozens of people whose lives this man had saved, at the careful way they watched him with a mixture of gratitude and worship that made her stomach clench with recognition. They knew he was more than human. They might not understand the nature of his gift, but they could see that Thomas could do things no ordinary healer could accomplish.

"I'm someone who knows what you are," she said quietly. "And I know what will happen if you continue on this path."

Thomas's eyes sharpened with sudden wariness. "What do you mean?"

Eleanor glanced at Augustine, who had remained near the entrance, watching the warehouse's other occupants for signs of danger. Then she reached out and grasped Thomas's hand.

The vision that flowed between them was different from what she had shared with Augustine. Where the monk's memories had been controlled and purposeful, Thomas's were chaotic, driven by exhaustion and the constant press of other people's pain. She saw his gift awakening during his youth, the way he had discovered he could draw sickness from animals, then people. She felt his growing compulsion to heal, the way each use of his power made it harder to resist the next opportunity to help someone in need.

But beneath his personal history, she showed him what she had seen in her own prophetic vision: the world burning, humanity destroying itself, the earth rejecting the species that had learned to transcend its own nature.

Thomas jerked his hand away, his face pale with shock. "That... that was real?"

"As real as your gift," Eleanor replied. "As real as the healing you've done here."

"But these people need help. I can save them. I can—"

"And word will spread," Augustine said, approaching now that the connection had been broken. "Stories will be told of the miracle healer of Dover. Pilgrims will come seeking impossible cures. Eventually, someone in authority will take notice, and they'll want to understand how you accomplish what you do."

Thomas looked around the warehouse, his gaze settling on faces he had pulled back from death's door. "So I should let them die? Let children suffer when I have the power to help them?"

Eleanor felt the familiar weight of the choice settling on her shoulders. In her vision, she had seen the paradise that the gifted could create—a world without suffering, without preventable death, without the arbitrary cruelties that marked human existence. But she had also seen what came after that paradise, when fear overcame wonder and humanity turned on its would-be saviors.

"Not all of them," she said finally. "You can help some, quietly, carefully. But you must learn to walk away from those you cannot save without exposing yourself."

"That's not a choice," Thomas said, his voice breaking. "That's torture."

"Yes," Eleanor agreed. "It is."

The silence that followed was broken by a commotion outside the warehouse. Voices shouting, the sound of running feet, the clatter of weapons. Augustine moved to the entrance and peered out, then returned with his face grim.

"City guards," he reported. "Someone has told them about the miracle healer."

Thomas struggled to his feet, swaying with exhaustion. "I won't abandon these people."

"You don't have to," Eleanor said, her mind racing through possibilities. "But you can't be here when the guards arrive. Augustine, is there another way out?"

"The back wall. There's a loose board that opens onto an alley."

Eleanor turned to the prostitute who had been guarding the entrance. "What's your name?"

"Mary," the woman replied.

"Mary, can you tend to the sick? Give them water, keep them comfortable?"

"I... I don't know how to heal like Thomas does."

"You don't need to heal them. You just need to be here when the guards arrive, to tell them that the healer left this morning, that he was just an ordinary physician who did what he could before moving on to the next city."

Mary nodded, understanding. "And Thomas?"

Eleanor looked at the man who had saved so many lives that he had nearly destroyed himself in the process. "Thomas comes with us. There are others like him who need to hear what we've learned."

"Others?" Thomas's eyes widened. "There are more people with gifts like mine?"

"Across all of Europe," Augustine confirmed. "And if we don't find them soon, if we don't convince them to hide what they are, the vision Eleanor showed you will become reality."

The sound of boots on cobblestones grew closer. Eleanor could hear the guards questioning people in the street, following the trail of stories about miraculous healings back to its source.

"Decide now," Eleanor said urgently. "Come with us and live to help others in secret, or stay here and risk exposing all of us."

Thomas looked one last time around the warehouse, at the people whose lives he had saved, at the children who would grow up healthy because of his sacrifice. Then he nodded and moved toward the back wall.

Augustine had already worked the loose board free, revealing a narrow passage into the alley beyond. They slipped through one by one, Eleanor going last. As she prepared to leave, she turned back to Mary.

"Tell them the healer was a traveling monk," she said. "Tell them he spoke of going to Canterbury to pray for the souls of the dead."

Mary smiled grimly. "I'll tell them he was touched by God, and that God called him elsewhere."

"Not God," Eleanor said quietly. "Something else entirely."

They emerged into the alley just as the guards reached the warehouse entrance. Eleanor could hear Mary's voice, explaining in worried tones that the holy man had left hours ago, that she didn't know where he had gone, that she was just trying to care for the sick as best she could.

Augustine led them through a maze of back streets and narrow passages, avoiding the main thoroughfares where guards might be searching. Thomas stumbled frequently, his body pushed beyond endurance, but he kept moving. It wasn't until they reached the outskirts of Dover that Eleanor allowed herself to believe they had escaped.

They took shelter in an abandoned chapel, its roof partially collapsed and its altar stone cracked by weather and neglect. Augustine shared bread and cheese from his pack while Eleanor tended to Thomas's exhaustion as best she could. She couldn't heal him the way he had healed others, but her touch seemed to ease some of his pain.

"How many others are there?" Thomas asked when he had recovered enough to speak clearly.

Eleanor closed her eyes and reached out with the sensitivity that had awakened during her contact with Augustine. The golden threads were clearer now, easier to follow. "In England alone? Perhaps two dozen. Across the continent..." She shook her head. "Hundreds, certainly. Maybe more."

"And they're all in danger of exposing themselves?"

"Different dangers," Augustine replied. "Some, like you, are driven by compassion to help others. Some are being used by those in power who don't fully understand what they're dealing with. Some are simply struggling to control abilities they don't comprehend."

Eleanor thought of the network she had glimpsed, of all those points of light scattered across a continent torn by war, plague, and superstition. Each one represented a person carrying a burden they hadn't chosen, making impossible choices between their own survival and their desire to use their gifts.

"There's a girl in Normandy," she said, drawing on the impressions she had gathered. "She can speak to animals, understand their thoughts. She's been helping her village track wolves and predict the weather, but people are starting to notice that she knows things she shouldn't."

"A blacksmith in the Germanic states can forge metal with his bare hands," Augustine added. "He's been crafting weapons and armor that are far superior to anything his peers can produce. His lord is beginning to ask questions about his methods."

"And in Italia," Eleanor continued, "there's a woman who can make herself invisible at will. She's been using her gift to steal food for the poor, but the authorities are growing suspicious of crimes that seem to have no perpetrator."

Thomas listened with growing amazement and horror. "All of them walking the same edge we walked tonight—between helping people and exposing themselves."

"Yes," Eleanor said. "And if even one of them is discovered, if their abilities become widely known, it could trigger the cascade that leads to the vision's fulfillment."

"So what do we do? How do we find them all?"

Eleanor stood and moved to the chapel's broken window, looking out at the star-filled sky. Somewhere out there, hundreds of people were struggling with gifts they didn't understand, making choices that could doom or save the world. The knowing in her chest told her that this was her purpose, the reason her abilities had awakened during humanity's darkest hour.

"We build a network," she said finally. "We find them one by one, show them what I showed you, and convince them to join us in hiding what we are."

"And if they refuse?" Augustine asked.

Eleanor remembered the look in Thomas's eyes when he had spoken of letting people die rather than exposing himself. The choice she was asking people to make wasn't just about hiding their abilities—it was about accepting a lifetime of watching suffering they could prevent, of restraining themselves when every instinct screamed at them to act.

"Then we hope they're strong enough to keep the secret anyway," she said. "And we pray that our vision was wrong."

But even as she spoke the words, Eleanor knew the vision hadn't been wrong. The future she had seen was as certain as sunrise, unless they could convince every gifted person in Europe to sacrifice their authenticity for the sake of humanity's survival.

It was an impossible task. But as she looked at Thomas and Augustine, both of whom had already made that terrible choice, Eleanor felt the first stirring of something that might have been hope.

"Where do we start?" Thomas asked.

Eleanor reached out with her developing sensitivity, following the golden threads that connected her to others like herself. The strongest signal came from the south and west, across the channel to the lands beyond.

"Francia," she said. "There's someone there, someone powerful. If we can convince her to join us, she might be able to help us reach the others."

Augustine nodded. "Marie Delacroix. She controls the weather itself. But she's been using her gift to protect her village from raiders. The local lord has taken notice."

"Then we'd better reach her before the wrong people do," Eleanor said.

As they prepared to rest for the remainder of the night, Eleanor found herself thinking about the warehouse they had left behind, about Mary tending to the sick without Thomas's miraculous healing power, about all the people who would die from preventable causes because the gifted were choosing to hide rather than help.

The weight of those deaths would rest on her shoulders, she knew. Every person who suffered while the gifted remained hidden, every disaster they could have prevented, every injustice they failed to correct—all of it would be part of the price of preventing the greater catastrophe.

But as she drifted off to sleep on the chapel's cold stone floor, Eleanor's last thought was of the vision's final image: that empty settlement at the end of all things, silence where humanity should have been. Whatever the cost of hiding, it was nothing compared to the price of revelation.

The covenant was growing, one impossible choice at a time.

CHAPTER 3: THE GATHERING

Six months later

The village of Beaumont-sur-Oise lay beneath a canopy of unnatural calm. While the surrounding countryside bore the scars of English raiders—burned fields, abandoned farmsteads, smoke rising from distant hamlets—this small settlement seemed to exist within a protective bubble. The wheat grew tall and golden despite the season's drought, the livestock grazed peacefully in pastures that should have been trampled by war horses, and the very air seemed to shimmer with an otherworldly stillness.

Eleanor stood at the edge of the village, feeling the familiar pulse of supernatural energy that had drawn them across the channel and through weeks of dangerous travel. Beside her, Augustine adjusted his monk's robes while Thomas checked the leather satchel that now contained their most precious possession: a collection of written testimonies from the twelve gifted individuals they had already found and convinced to join their covenant.

"She knows we're here," Eleanor said, her enhanced senses picking up the subtle shift in the air currents around them. "She's been watching us since we crested the hill."

"Can you sense her mood?" Augustine asked.

Eleanor closed her eyes and extended her awareness, following the golden thread that connected her to the village's protector. "Suspicious. Protective. And..." She paused, frowning. "Afraid. But not of us. Of something else."

They made their way down the dirt path toward Beaumont-sur-Oise, passing farmers who watched them with the wary eyes of people who had learned to distrust strangers. But Eleanor noticed something else in their gazes—a confidence that seemed out of place in these war-torn lands, as if these villagers knew they possessed protection that no earthly army could breach.

The village square was dominated by a small stone church and a well that appeared to never run dry despite the drought. Eleanor could feel the supernatural influence most strongly here, as if the very stones had been blessed by otherworldly power. A woman emerged from the church as they approached—tall and elegant, perhaps twenty-five years old, with auburn hair that seemed to move in breezes that touched no one else.

"Travelers," she said, her voice carrying the musical cadence of educated French. "I am Marie Delacroix. Welcome to Beaumont-sur-Oise. Though I wonder what brings a monk, a healer, and a..." she studied Eleanor with eyes the color of storm clouds, "...a seer to our humble village."

Eleanor felt Thomas tense beside her. In the months since Dover, they had developed careful approaches for making contact with the gifted, but Marie's immediate recognition of their nature suggested this conversation would be unlike any they'd had before.

"We've come to speak with you about a vision," Eleanor said simply. "About choices that must be made, and prices that must be paid."

Marie's expression didn't change, but the wind that had been playing through her hair stilled completely. "Perhaps we should speak privately. There is a glade beyond the village where we will not be overheard."

She led them past the last houses and into a grove of oak trees that seemed older than memory. Here, away from curious eyes, Marie allowed her true nature to show. The air around her danced with visible currents, leaves spiraled in impossible patterns, and when she gestured, clouds gathered overhead despite the clear sky.

"You are not the first to seek me out," she said without preamble. "Three months ago, agents of the Duke of Normandy came asking questions about the village's unusual prosperity. Last month, it was English spies trying to understand why their raids consistently fail in this region. And now you three, carrying secrets that taste of power similar to my own."

Eleanor stepped forward, extending her hand. "May I show you what I've seen?"

Marie studied her for a long moment, then nodded. "Very well. But know that if you attempt to harm me, the wind itself will tear you apart."

The moment their skin touched, Eleanor felt the rush of connection that had become familiar over the past months. But Marie's mind was unlike any she had encountered—organized like a vast library, with memories sorted by season and emotion catalogued like weather patterns. Through this orderly consciousness, Eleanor shared her vision of the future: the paradise and the catastrophe, the choice between revelation and concealment, the price of either path.

Marie gasped and pulled her hand away, her control slipping enough that a sudden gust scattered leaves around them like snow.

"My God," she whispered. "That was... that was real?"

"As real as the drought you've been holding back," Augustine said gently. "As real as the protection you've given this village."

Marie sank onto a fallen log, her hands shaking. "I thought... I hoped my gifts were a blessing. A chance to help my people survive these terrible times."

"They are a blessing," Thomas said, his voice thick with understanding. "But blessings can become curses if they draw the wrong attention."

"The Duke's men," Marie said slowly. "They've been asking more specific questions lately. About unnatural weather patterns, about villages that seem immune to the troubles plaguing the rest of the region." She looked up at Eleanor with eyes that now held the same haunted knowledge they all carried. "How long before they conclude that something supernatural protects us?"

"Days, perhaps weeks," Eleanor admitted. "Your protection of this village has been beautiful, but it's also been visible. The pattern of your interventions creates a trail that anyone with eyes can follow."

Marie stood abruptly, beginning to pace among the oak trees. "So you want me to stop? To let the raiders come, to watch my people suffer and die when I have the power to prevent it?"

"We want you to be more careful," Augustine said. "Help when you can do so without creating obvious supernatural effects. Allow some natural disasters to occur. Make your interventions look like luck rather than miracles."

"And when my people die because I held back?" Marie's voice rose, and thunder rumbled overhead despite the clear sky. "What then?"

Eleanor felt the familiar weight of the impossible choice settling over the glade. This was the moment that defined every recruitment—when the gifted person truly understood what the covenant required of them.

"Then you live with their deaths," Eleanor said quietly. "As we all do. As I did when I walked away from my village while people still died of plague. As Thomas does every time he chooses not to heal someone who might be saved."

Thomas nodded, his face grave. "The first time you let someone die when you could have saved them, you'll think it will destroy you. But you'll survive. And then it will happen again, and again, until you learn to carry that weight without breaking."

Marie stared at them both with something approaching horror. "That's not living. That's existing as a ghost of what you could be."

"Yes," Eleanor agreed. "But it's existence that preserves the possibility of a future. The alternative is the paradise we showed you, followed by extinction."

For long minutes, the only sound in the glade was the whisper of wind through leaves—natural wind, not summoned by Marie's gift. Eleanor could feel the struggle taking place in the other woman's mind, the war between compassion and survival, between the desire to help and the need to hide.

Finally, Marie spoke. "There are others, aren't there? Others who have made this choice?"

Augustine opened the leather satchel and withdrew several carefully written documents. "Twelve so far. A healer in Scotland who can cure any poison. A woman in the Germanic states who can speak with the dead. A man in Iberia who can become invisible at will. Each of them struggling with the same decision you face now."

Marie read through the testimonies, her expression growing more troubled with each account. "They all agreed? All of them chose to hide rather than help?"

"Not all immediately," Thomas admitted. "Some required more convincing. Some needed to see the vision for themselves before they believed. But yes, eventually they all chose concealment over revelation."

"And if I refuse? If I decide that the risk is worth taking, that the good I can do outweighs the danger?"

Eleanor felt the weight of the question settle in her chest. In the months since leaving Ravenscroft, they had encountered three gifted individuals who had refused to join the covenant. She tried not to think about what had happened to them.

"Then you become a danger to all of us," she said honestly. "Your exposure would validate stories about the others. Your capture would lead to questions about abilities like yours. Your very existence as a known supernatural being makes the future we showed you more likely to occur."

The threat hung unspoken in the air between them. Marie was intelligent enough to understand what Eleanor wasn't saying—that the covenant had developed ways of dealing with those who refused to maintain secrecy.

"I need time to consider," Marie said finally.

"Time we may not have," Augustine warned. "The Duke's investigation is advancing. If you're going to disappear from this region, it must be soon."

"Disappear?" Marie's voice sharpened. "You want me to abandon my people entirely?"

"We want you to step back gradually," Eleanor explained. "Let natural disasters begin to affect the village again. Allow the raiders to achieve some small successes. Make it appear that whatever protection you've been providing is fading naturally. Then, when the Duke's men find nothing supernatural to investigate, you can return to helping in smaller, more careful ways."

Marie walked to the edge of the glade, staring back toward the village where people were going about their daily lives, secure in the protection she had provided. "And if the raiders kill people during this transition? If children die in storms I could have prevented?"

"Then you save hundreds of thousands by sacrificing dozens," Thomas said bluntly. "It's not a fair trade. It's not a good trade. But it's the only trade that prevents the vision from becoming reality."

Eleanor watched Marie struggle with the decision, feeling the familiar mixture of sympathy and urgency that had marked every recruitment. They couldn't force her to join—forced compliance was too unreliable—but they also couldn't afford to leave without an answer.

The choice was made for them by the sound of horses approaching through the forest. Augustine moved to the edge of the glade and peered through the trees, then returned with his face grim.

"Armed men," he reported. "Flying the Duke's banner. They're heading for the village."

Marie's expression hardened with resolve. "How many?"

"Twenty, perhaps thirty."

Marie closed her eyes, and Eleanor felt the gathering of supernatural power around them. Clouds began to form overhead, and the wind picked up with unnatural speed.

"Marie, no," Eleanor said urgently. "This is exactly what will expose you."

"I won't let them hurt my people."

The first drops of rain began to fall, but they were warm—too warm for the season—and they fell in patterns that defied natural weather. Eleanor could sense Marie's power reaching out across the countryside, calling storms that would turn the roads to mud and send the raiders seeking shelter instead of pillage.

"Stop," Eleanor commanded, reaching out and grasping Marie's arm. "Let me show you one more thing."

This time, the vision Eleanor shared was not of the distant future, but of the immediate consequences of Marie's choices. She showed her the Duke's men taking note of the unnatural storm, the reports that would be filed, the investigations that would follow. She showed her the inevitable conclusion: Marie discovered, captured, studied like an animal in a cage while other members of the covenant were hunted down one by one.

Marie jerked away from the contact, but the storm she had been summoning dissipated. The unnatural clouds broke apart, the warm rain stopped, and normal weather patterns resumed.

"You're asking me to watch my people suffer," she said, tears streaming down her face.

"I'm asking you to let some suffer so that all might survive," Eleanor replied. "It's the choice we all have to make."

From the direction of the village came the sound of shouting—not the screams of attack, but the calls of men organizing a defense. Marie's people had learned to protect themselves in more conventional ways as well.

"They'll fight," Augustine observed. "Not all protection has to be supernatural."

Marie watched the glade entrance, listening to the distant sounds of conflict. When the shouting died down after perhaps an hour, she closed her eyes and reached out with senses beyond the ordinary.

"The raiders withdrew," she said finally. "The village militia drove them off."

"Without supernatural intervention," Thomas pointed out. "Your people are stronger than you think."

Marie was quiet for a long time, staring at the spot where her summoned clouds had been. When she finally spoke, her voice carried the weight of terrible understanding.

"If I join your covenant, what exactly would that mean? What would be required of me?"

Eleanor felt a mixture of relief and sorrow as she heard the acceptance in Marie's tone. Another recruitment was nearing success, but at the cost of another person's innocence and hope.

"You would need to leave this region for a time," Augustine explained. "Establish yourself somewhere else, under a different identity. Learn to help people in ways that don't create obvious patterns of supernatural intervention."

"And in return?"

"In return, you become part of a network," Eleanor said. "Others who understand what you've sacrificed, who can provide support when the weight of inaction becomes too heavy to bear alone."

Marie nodded slowly. "And if I agree to this, you'll help me protect my people during the transition? Ensure they're not defenseless when I step back?"

"We'll do what we can," Thomas promised. "There are ways to help that don't involve obvious supernatural intervention."

As the sun began to set through the oak trees, Marie made her choice. "I'll join your covenant. God help me, I'll join, and I'll learn to let people die when I could save them."

Eleanor felt no victory in the moment, only the familiar sadness that came with each recruitment. Another person had chosen to sacrifice their authentic nature for the sake of humanity's survival. Another light had agreed to hide itself under a bushel.

But as they prepared to leave the glade, Eleanor's enhanced senses picked up something new—distant golden threads, stronger than any she had detected before.

"There are others," she said suddenly. "Powerful ones. In Italia and the northern lands."

Augustine followed her gaze toward the southern horizon. "Giovanni Torriani. He crafts with fire itself, creating works of art and weaponry that surpass anything natural skill could achieve."

"And in the north?" Marie asked, her practical mind already adapting to her new role in the covenant.

"Bjorn Eriksson," Eleanor replied, feeling the distant pulse of barely contained strength. "He possesses the power of twenty men, but he's been using it openly. There are stories spreading across the northern seas about the warrior who cannot be killed."

Marie gathered her few possessions, taking one last look toward the village she would soon have to protect in smaller, more careful ways. "How many more will we need to find?"

"All of them," Eleanor said simply. "Every gifted person in Europe must choose between revelation and concealment. We cannot afford to leave even one free to expose the rest."

As they left the glade and began planning their journey south toward Italia, Eleanor reflected on how much their small group had grown. What had begun as her and Augustine was now four people bound together by shared knowledge and mutual sacrifice. Soon it would be five, then six, then as many as it took to ensure that the vision never became reality.

The covenant was no longer just an idea—it was becoming a living network of people who had chosen to live as shadows so that humanity might survive in the light.

But with each recruitment, Eleanor felt the weight of leadership growing heavier. These people looked to her for guidance, for reassurance that their sacrifices were worthwhile. And sometimes, in her darker moments, she wondered if they were building something noble or merely becoming a organization dedicated to suppressing the very gifts that could make the world a better place.

Those doubts would have to wait. There were others to find, others to convince, others to bind with the same terrible choice that had claimed them all.

The gathering continued.

CHAPTER 4: THE FIRST TEST

Two months after Beaumont-sur-Oise

The city of Reims rose before them like a monument to human suffering. Even from a distance of several miles, the smoke was visible—not the clean smoke of hearth fires, but the thick, oily columns that rose from the burning pyres where the dead were consumed by the hundreds. The Great Mortality had found the cathedral city with a vengeance, and from the reports they had gathered in roadside taverns, nearly half the population had already succumbed.

Eleanor stood on the hill overlooking the city, feeling the familiar ache in her chest that came whenever she encountered suffering she had the power to alleviate. Beside her, the six members of their growing covenant maintained a grim silence. What had begun as her desperate alliance with Augustine had become something larger—a network of the gifted who had chosen concealment over revelation, secrecy over service.

"We should go around," Thomas said quietly, his healer's instincts warring with the discipline they had all learned. "There's nothing for us here but temptation."

"Nothing but people dying who could be saved," Marcus Aurelius corrected, his voice carrying the slight accent of his Roman birth. Of all their recruits, Marcus had been the most difficult to convince, and even now, months after joining them, Eleanor could sense his resistance to their covenant's restrictions.

Augustine shifted uncomfortably in his monk's robes. "Marcus, we've discussed this. Cities in the grip of plague are precisely the situations we must avoid. Too many witnesses, too much desperation. People notice miracles when they're surrounded by death."

Marcus stepped forward, his tall frame tense with barely contained energy. Eleanor could feel the power radiating from him—a gift that defied easy categorization. Where Thomas could heal through touch and Marie could command the weather, Marcus possessed something more fundamental: the ability to impose his will upon reality itself. He could cure diseases with a word, mend broken bones with a gesture, even restore life to the recently dead.

It was precisely the sort of overwhelming power that made concealment both necessary and nearly impossible.

"Look at them," Marcus said, pointing toward the city where ant-like figures could be seen carrying bodies to the burning grounds. "Thousands of people suffering and dying while we stand here debating the wisdom of helping them. What good is power if we never use it?"

Eleanor felt the familiar weight of leadership settling on her shoulders. In the months since their covenant had begun to grow, she had become the final arbiter of such disputes—the one who decided when their gifts could be used and when they must remain hidden. It was a responsibility she had never sought and one that grew heavier with each person they recruited.

"The good," she said carefully, "is that we continue to exist. That our gifts remain secret. That the future I showed you all doesn't come to pass."

"Your vision," Marcus said, turning to face her with eyes that burned with frustrated compassion, "showed what might happen if the gifted were revealed. But we don't know that revelation would automatically lead to catastrophe. Perhaps humanity would welcome our help. Perhaps the paradise you glimpsed could exist without the destruction that followed."

Marie, who had grown quieter and more thoughtful since leaving her village's protection to chance, shook her head. "You didn't feel what Eleanor showed us, Marcus. The fear in people's minds when they realized what we could do. The inevitability of that fear turning to hatred."

"But that was one possible future among many," Marcus insisted. "Eleanor herself has said that prophecy is fluid, that choices can change outcomes. What if the choice to help, to reveal ourselves in service to humanity, creates a different future than the one she saw?"

Eleanor closed her eyes and reached out with her prophetic senses, trying to pierce the veil of possibility that surrounded their current situation. The future branched before them like a vast tree, each decision creating new pathways, new potential outcomes. She could see fragments—glimpses of what might occur depending on their choices here.

In some visions, they skirted the city and continued their journey unmolested. In others, Marcus broke from the group and used his powers openly, creating ripples that spread outward like stones cast into still water. But the endings of those visions remained frustratingly unclear, lost in the chaos of too many variables to calculate.

"I can't see clearly," she admitted finally. "There are too many possibilities, too many choices that could alter the outcome."

Marcus seized on her uncertainty. "Then we proceed with caution but not cowardice. I propose a compromise—we enter the city quietly, and I use my abilities to heal small numbers of people in areas where word won't spread quickly. The poor quarters, the forgotten corners where no one pays attention to another minor miracle."

"No," Eleanor said immediately. "Any use of your gift in a place like this creates risk. The desperate notice everything, Marcus. They cling to hope wherever they can find it."

"And if I do nothing? If we walk past this city while thousands die from a plague I could end with a few hours' work?" Marcus's voice rose, and several of their companions stepped back instinctively. When Marcus was agitated, reality itself seemed to shimmer around him, as if the world was uncertain whether to obey natural law or his will.

Thomas moved to stand beside Eleanor, his own struggles with similar choices evident in his haggard features. "I understand the temptation, Marcus. Every day I choose not to heal someone is another weight on my soul. But the alternative—"

"The alternative is that we become gods walking among mortals!" Marcus interrupted. "And perhaps that's what we're meant to be. Perhaps our gifts are meant to elevate humanity, not hide from it."

The words hung in the air like a challenge. Eleanor felt the familiar chill that came whenever someone questioned the fundamental premise of their covenant. She had seen this moment in visions— the first serious challenge to their unity, the first crack that could widen into the very schism her prophetic sight had warned her about.

"If we become gods," she said quietly, "then we become targets. And when humanity turns on its gods, the destruction is absolute."

Marcus was quiet for a long moment, staring at the smoke rising from Reims. When he spoke again, his voice carried a new note of decision that made Eleanor's prophetic senses scream in warning.

"You're asking me to be complicit in genocide," he said. "To stand by and watch an entire city die when I have the power to save it. I cannot—I will not—make that choice."

"Marcus—" Augustine began, but the Roman was already moving down the hill toward the city.

"Don't follow me," he called back. "I'll not force your complicity in my choice. But neither will I be bound by your fears."

Eleanor felt the moment of crisis crystallizing around them. She could let Marcus go and hope he would be careful, preserving the unity of their group at the cost of an unknown risk. Or she could use her authority as their informal leader to stop him, potentially fracturing their covenant in a different way.

"Marie," she said urgently, "can you—"

"Create a storm to stop him?" Marie finished. "Use my power openly, in view of the city, to prevent him from using his?" She shook her head. "That would defeat the purpose."

Eleanor watched Marcus reach the city's outskirts, her prophetic senses churning with fragmentary visions of what his choice might unleash. Most of the possibilities were chaotic, impossible to interpret clearly, but one image came through with terrifying clarity: Marcus standing in Reims' central square, his hands raised to heaven, calling on power that made the very air burn with supernatural light.

"We have to follow him," she decided. "Try to limit the damage."

They made their way down the hill and into the city's outer districts, following the trail Marcus had left through Eleanor's supernatural senses. Reims was a city transformed by plague—streets that should have bustled with merchants and pilgrims were nearly empty, buildings stood abandoned with doors hanging open, and the few people they encountered moved with the shuffling gait of those who had given up hope.

Eleanor found Marcus in the poverty-stricken quarter near the city's eastern wall, where the plague had hit hardest and traditional healers had long since fled or died. He stood in a narrow alley surrounded by a dozen plague victims in various stages of the disease, his hands glowing with subtle light as he moved from person to person.

"Marcus, stop," Eleanor hissed, ducking into the alley behind him. "You're being too obvious."

"Am I?" Marcus didn't turn around, focused instead on the child in his arms whose breathing had already begun to ease. "These people are dying. All of them. And I can save them with no more effort than it takes to speak their names."

Eleanor watched in fascination and horror as Marcus worked. His gift was unlike anything she had encountered—not the targeted healing Thomas provided or the environmental manipulation Marie could achieve, but something fundamental. He seemed to be rewriting reality itself, declaring that these people were healthy and having the universe agree with his assessment.

"Even if no one notices immediately," Augustine said from the alley's entrance, where he was keeping watch, "the pattern will become obvious. A dozen people miraculously recover in the same location? Word will spread."

"Let it spread," Marcus said, moving to the next victim. "Let people know that hope exists, that death is not inevitable."

As if summoned by his words, a commotion erupted from the street beyond the alley. Eleanor heard voices raised in excitement, the sound of running feet, the growing murmur of a crowd discovering something impossible.

"Too late," Thomas muttered.

Eleanor peered around the alley's corner and saw what she had feared most: witnesses. A group of pilgrims who had been passing through the district had seen Marcus's work, and now they were spreading word throughout the neighborhood. She could hear fragments of their excited chatter—talk of miracles, of divine intervention, of a holy man who could cure the plague with a touch.

"Marcus, we need to leave. Now."

But Marcus was deep in his work, his consciousness focused entirely on the sick people around him. Eleanor could feel the power flowing through him like a river in flood, vast and barely controlled. Each healing seemed to strengthen rather than drain him, as if the act of imposing his will upon reality only made that will more potent.

"Marcus!" she said more urgently.

This time he heard her, turning with eyes that seemed to burn with inner light. "I can save them all, Eleanor. Everyone in this city. The plague would end in a single day."

Eleanor felt her prophetic senses screaming in alarm. She reached out and grasped Marcus's arm, forcing a vision-touch that showed him what she could see: crowds gathering, word spreading beyond the district, authorities taking notice. And beneath it all, the golden threads that connected the gifted beginning to pulse with danger as the secret they all shared came under threat.

Marcus jerked away from her touch, but the vision had done its work. The burning light in his eyes dimmed, and for the first time since entering the city, he seemed to truly see their situation.

"How long do we have?" he asked.

"Minutes," Augustine reported from his watch position. "The crowd is growing. I can see city guards approaching."

Eleanor looked around the alley at the people Marcus had saved—men, women, and children who moments ago had been dying and now stood healthy and whole. Their gratitude was obvious, but so was their amazement. These were not subtle healings that could be attributed to natural recovery. They were obvious, undeniable miracles.

"We run," she decided. "All of us, together. Marie, can you create a distraction?"

Marie nodded and closed her eyes. Within moments, a sudden wind picked up throughout the district, strong enough to knock people off balance and send debris flying. In the confusion, Eleanor's group managed to slip away from the alley and make their way toward the city's northern gate.

But as they moved through the streets, Eleanor could hear the story spreading behind them. The tale was already growing in the telling—a holy man who could cure any disease, who had brought the dead back to life, who had performed miracles that surpassed even the saints of old.

They reached the city gate just as the pursuit began in earnest. Eleanor could hear the sound of horses being readied, of search parties organizing, of authorities mobilizing to find the miracle worker who had vanished into the crowd.

"They'll search every road, every village," Thomas said as they hurried into the countryside beyond Reims. "Word will spread to other cities, other regions."

"And when the stories reach the church authorities or the royal court?" Augustine asked.

Eleanor didn't need her prophetic gift to answer that question. She had seen it in her vision-touch with Marcus—interrogations, investigations, the systematic hunting of anyone with unusual abilities. The very thing their covenant existed to prevent.

"We'll need to split up," she decided. "Scatter across different regions, maintain minimal contact until this dies down."

Marcus, who had been silent since their escape, finally spoke. "This is my fault. I'll draw their attention away from the rest of you."

"We stay together," Eleanor said firmly. "Whatever the consequences, we face them as a group."

But even as she spoke the words, Eleanor's prophetic senses were showing her glimpses of what those consequences might be. Wanted notices posted in every major city. Rewards offered for information about the miracle healer. The systematic persecution of anyone who showed unusual abilities or knowledge.

They had survived their first test, but barely. And in surviving, they had learned the terrible truth that Eleanor's vision had tried to show them: even the most careful exposure could spiral into catastrophe with frightening speed.

As they put distance between themselves and Reims, Eleanor found herself walking beside Marcus, who seemed diminished somehow, as if the effort of containing his power again after releasing it so fully had cost him something essential.

"The people I healed," he said quietly. "Do you think they'll suffer for what I did? When the authorities come looking for explanations?"

Eleanor's heart clenched at the question. In her rush to prevent greater exposure, she hadn't considered the fate of those Marcus had saved. Now, with the perspective of distance, she could see the cruel irony: the very people he had tried to help might become targets of suspicion and persecution.

"I don't know," she admitted. "But that's why we have the covenant, Marcus. That's why we hide. Every action we take, no matter how well-intentioned, creates ripples that can hurt innocent people."

Marcus nodded slowly, the last of his resistance to their rules dying in the face of harsh reality. "I understand now. The price of our gifts isn't just what we sacrifice by hiding them. It's what others pay when we don't."

As the sun set behind them and the lights of Reims faded into the distance, Eleanor reflected on what they had learned. Their covenant was stronger now, tempered by the first real test of their resolve. But it was also more fragile, held together by the shared knowledge of how quickly their careful balance could collapse.

The gathering phase of their mission was over. Now came the harder task: learning to live with the weight of their choices, and teaching others to do the same.

Behind them, the city of Reims burned with stories of miracles and wonder. Ahead lay a future where such stories would have to be carefully suppressed, transformed into legends and myths that posed no threat to those who carried the real power.

The covenant had survived its first test. But Eleanor knew it would not be the last.

CHAPTER 5: THE COVENANT BORN

Three weeks after Reims

The monastery of Saint-Wandrille rose from the Norman countryside like a finger of stone pointed toward heaven, its ancient walls scarred by centuries of weather and war. Founded in the seventh century by a Frankish nobleman who had abandoned worldly power for spiritual pursuits, it had endured Viking raids, political upheavals, and the slow erosion of time itself. Now, in the dying months of 1348, it served as sanctuary for a different kind of gathering—one that would echo through generations yet unborn.

Eleanor stood in the monastery's scriptorium, watching the late afternoon light filter through windows of precious glass, casting rainbow patterns across the stone floor. Around her, the seven members of their covenant moved quietly among the ancient texts, each lost in private contemplation of what they were about to undertake. The formal creation of their pact—the binding agreement that would govern not just their own lives, but the lives of their children and their children's children.

Brother Anselm, the monastery's aging librarian, had provided them with sanctuary and materials in exchange for Marcus's discrete healing of the arthritis that had plagued him for decades. The old monk asked no questions about their true nature, content to believe they were scholarly pilgrims seeking a quiet place to compose religious texts. In a way, Eleanor reflected, that wasn't entirely untrue. They were creating something sacred, though perhaps not in the way Brother Anselm imagined.

"The parchment is prepared," Augustine announced, setting down his quill after hours of careful work. His months of traveling with Eleanor had honed his ability to craft documents that looked appropriately official, complete with religious flourishes that would make their covenant appear to be a legitimate religious order should it ever be discovered.

Eleanor approached the table where Augustine had been working, studying the document that would define their shared future. Written in Latin and illuminated with the sort of decorative script found in the finest religious manuscripts, it appeared to be the founding charter of a new monastic order dedicated to charitable works and spiritual contemplation. But beneath the traditional language lay the true purpose of their gathering.

"Read it aloud," Marie requested, her voice carrying the weight of someone about to make an irrevocable decision. Since joining them, she had grown more serious, more thoughtful, as if the magnitude of their mission had settled into her bones.

Augustine cleared his throat and began to read:

"In nomine Patris, et Filii, et Spiritus Sancti. In this year of our Lord 1348, we, the undersigned, do hereby establish a covenant of silence and service, binding ourselves and our bloodlines to the protection of humanity through the concealment of gifts that surpass mortal understanding."

Eleanor felt a familiar chill as the formal words gave weight to the choice they had all made individually. Around the table, she could see the same recognition in the faces of her companions—the understanding that they were crossing a threshold from which there could be no return.

Augustine continued: "We swear by our immortal souls to hide the abilities we have been granted, to use them only in service of the greater good and only when such use cannot be detected or traced to supernatural intervention. We bind our descendants to this same obligation, ensuring that knowledge of our gifts passes only through blood, and only to those who demonstrate both the ability to bear such knowledge and the wisdom to honor these restrictions."

Thomas stepped forward, his healer's hands steady despite the magnitude of the moment. "I, Thomas of Ashford, do solemnly swear to uphold this covenant. I bind my bloodline to secrecy, sacrificing the open use of my gift so that humanity might survive its own fear of what it cannot understand."

One by one, each member of their group stepped forward to make the same declaration. Marie pledged her weather-calling abilities to concealment. Marcus, still subdued by the consequences of his actions in Reims, swore to hide the reality-shaping power that could remake the world. Giovanni, the Italian fire-shaper they had recruited after Marie, promised to keep his gift hidden despite the

71

wonders he could create. The others followed—each taking the oath that would govern their lives and the lives of their descendants for generations to come.

When it came Eleanor's turn, she hesitated for a moment at the table, her hand poised above the parchment. In her prophetic sight, she could see the threads of possibility radiating out from this moment like spokes of an immense wheel. Each signature, each commitment, locked certain futures into place while closing off others. The weight of shaping destiny through the stroke of a pen was almost overwhelming.

But there was something else—something that made her hesitate even as the others waited expectantly. In the depths of her vision-sight, she could perceive a truth that none of the others suspected: the future she had shown them all, the catastrophic revelation that would doom humanity, was only one of several possible endings she had witnessed.

The other visions were harder to interpret, clouded by the complexity of choices not yet made and consequences not yet understood. But in those alternative futures, she glimpsed a different kind of catastrophe—one that arose not from the revelation of supernatural gifts, but from their continued concealment. She saw the gifted consuming themselves from within, their abilities growing stronger with each generation of suppression until they could no longer be contained. She saw the covenant fracturing under the weight of inherited guilt and enforced secrecy. She saw a civil war among the supernatural that would make the revelation-catastrophe seem merciful by comparison.

The question that haunted her was simple: which future was more likely to come to pass?

Eleanor's prophetic gift had shown her that the act of observation itself could influence outcomes. By revealing one catastrophic future to her companions, she had made them less likely to choose the path that led to it. But if she revealed the alternative catastrophe—the one that arose from following the very covenant they were about to formalize—would she be steering them toward the revelation-future she feared even more?

"Eleanor?" Augustine's voice broke through her internal struggle. "Are you prepared to take the oath?"

She looked around the table at the faces of people who had become more than allies—they had become family, bound together by shared secrets and mutual sacrifice. Each of them had given up something essential to be here, had chosen concealment over authenticity, had accepted a lifetime of watching suffering they could prevent. They trusted her judgment, relied on her prophetic sight to guide their choices.

How could she tell them that her sight had shown her multiple possible dooms, and that she wasn't certain which path would lead to salvation?

"I, Eleanor Blackthorne," she said finally, her voice steady despite the turmoil in her heart, "do solemnly swear to uphold this covenant.

I bind my bloodline to secrecy, using my gift of prophecy to guide our cause while ensuring that knowledge of our abilities never threatens the survival of humanity itself."

The words felt like lead in her mouth, heavy with the weight of the truth she was choosing not to reveal. But as she signed her name to the parchment with Augustine's carefully prepared ink, Eleanor told herself that she was making the only choice possible. The revelation-future she had shown the others was immediate and certain—within a generation, humanity would destroy itself if the gifted were exposed. The concealment-future was distant and uncertain, dependent on choices that might never be made and circumstances that might never arise.

Better to prevent the certain catastrophe and deal with the uncertain one if it ever materialized.

"It is done," Augustine said, sprinkling sand over the wet ink to help it dry. "The Covenant of Shadows is formally established."

"The Covenant of Shadows?" Marie asked, raising an eyebrow at the name Augustine had given their organization.

"We are the shadows cast by humanity's light," Augustine explained. "Present but unseen, protecting from the darkness while never claiming credit for our service."

Eleanor nodded, finding unexpected comfort in the metaphor. Shadows were necessary—they provided relief from harsh light, definition to objects that might otherwise seem flat and lifeless. But shadows also concealed, obscured, made it difficult to see clearly. Perhaps that was fitting for a group dedicated to hiding the truth about their own nature.

Marcus rolled the parchment carefully and sealed it with wax, pressing his signet ring into the soft material to create an official-looking mark. "Where will we keep it?"

"Here, for now," Augustine decided. "Brother Anselm has agreed to place it in the monastery's archives, where it will be preserved with other religious documents. If any of us die, the survivors can retrieve it. If we all die..." He shrugged. "Perhaps future generations will find it and understand what we tried to accomplish."

The practical arrangements continued as evening approached. They would scatter again, each taking a different route away from the monastery to avoid creating patterns that might be noticed. Eleanor would return to England, Thomas would travel north to Scotland, Marie would establish herself in a new region of Francia. They would maintain contact through a network of coded letters left at predetermined locations—monasteries, mostly, where Augustine's connections could ensure secure delivery.

But as they prepared to part ways, perhaps forever, Eleanor felt compelled to share at least part of the burden she carried.

"Before we separate," she said, drawing the group's attention, "there's something you should know about prophecy. About the nature of seeing the future."

The others gathered around her, sensing the gravity in her tone.

"Visions are not fixed," she continued carefully. "They show what is likely to occur if current patterns continue, but they can be changed by knowledge and choice. The future I showed you all—the catastrophe that comes from revelation—that future becomes less likely every time someone chooses concealment over exposure."

Thomas frowned. "Are you saying our covenant might prevent the catastrophe entirely?"

"I'm saying that prophecy is a conversation between possibility and choice," Eleanor replied, choosing her words with extreme care. "The future changes as we make decisions based on what we've seen. But that also means..." She paused, struggling with how much to reveal. "It means that new possibilities can emerge. Futures we haven't seen yet, consequences we haven't anticipated."

Augustine studied her face with the shrewd intelligence that had made him such an effective finder of the gifted. "You're warning us that success might bring its own dangers."

"I'm reminding you that vigilance must be eternal," Eleanor said, which was true even if it wasn't the complete truth. "Each generation must be prepared to face new challenges, to make their own choices about how to honor our covenant."

She could see understanding dawn in their faces—not complete understanding, but enough to plant the seeds of future flexibility. If her descendants ever faced the concealment-catastrophe she had glimpsed, perhaps they would remember her words and realize that the covenant might need to evolve to meet new circumstances.

It wasn't the full truth, but it was as much truth as she dared share without undermining the unity they had worked so hard to build.

As the sun set through the monastery's ancient windows, casting long shadows across the scriptorium floor, the seven members of the Covenant of Shadows prepared to begin their separate journeys. They had created something unprecedented—a network of the supernatural dedicated to its own concealment, a conspiracy of the gifted against their own revelation.

Eleanor embraced each of them in turn, knowing that she might never see some of them again. The covenant would continue through letters and occasional meetings, through the children they would raise and the secrets they would pass down, but the intimacy of shared discovery and mutual choice would fade into memory.

Thomas was the last to leave, pausing at the scriptorium door to look back at Eleanor with concern in his eyes.

"You're carrying something you haven't shared with us," he said quietly. "I can see it in the way you hesitate before speaking, the way you choose your words so carefully."

Eleanor felt her heart clench with the desire to tell him everything— about the multiple futures she had seen, about the impossible choice between catastrophes, about the fear that they might be preventing one doom only to ensure another. But the words wouldn't come. The risk was too great, the consequences too unpredictable.

"We're all carrying burdens now," she said instead. "That's the price of what we've undertaken."

Thomas nodded slowly, accepting her deflection even if he didn't entirely believe it. "If you ever need to share that burden, Eleanor, remember that you're not alone. The covenant binds us together even when we're apart."

After he left, Eleanor remained in the scriptorium as darkness fell and the monastery settled into evening prayers. Brother Anselm had left candles for her use, and in their flickering light, she opened her mind to her prophetic gift one final time before beginning her journey home.

The visions came slowly, cautiously, as if her sight was reluctant to reveal more than she could bear. She saw fragments of possible futures—her descendants struggling with the weight of inherited secrets, the covenant evolving and adapting to new circumstances, moments of crisis when the careful balance between concealment and service would be tested.

But beneath it all, threading through every possible timeline like a river flowing toward an inevitable sea, she sensed the approaching moment when her carefully hidden truth would finally be revealed. Someday, perhaps generations hence, her descendants would learn about the other catastrophe she had seen. They would understand that the choice between revelation and concealment was not as simple as she had made it seem.

When that moment came, they would have to make their own decision about which future to embrace. Eleanor could only hope that she had given them the tools they needed to choose wisely.

Rising from her chair, Eleanor extinguished the candles and made her way to the small cell Brother Anselm had provided for her use. Tomorrow she would begin the long journey back to England, back to a life of careful service and constant vigilance. But tonight, she allowed herself a moment of satisfaction at what they had accomplished.

The Covenant of Shadows was born. The gifted had chosen secrecy over revelation, service over recognition, survival over authenticity. For now, that would have to be enough.

Outside her window, the Norman countryside lay peaceful under starlight, unaware that it had just witnessed the creation of a conspiracy that would shape the hidden history of the world for centuries to come. In monasteries and manor houses, in villages and cities across Europe, the gifted would now begin the long work of learning to live as shadows—present but unseen, powerful but silent, guardians of a humanity that would never know their names.

The gathering was complete. The covenant was established. The long vigil had begun.

But deep in her heart, Eleanor carried the weight of the secret she had not shared—the knowledge that even the most carefully crafted plan could not account for every possible future, and that the choices they had made tonight might someday require their descendants to choose again, perhaps even to choose differently.

The covenant was born in shadow and secrecy. Whether it would die the same way remained to be seen.

CHAPTER 6: THE MINISTER'S BURDEN

Salem Village, Massachusetts

February 1692

Reverend Matthias Ashford stood at his pulpit, gazing out at the congregation that had gathered for morning worship despite the bitter February cold. Their faces, illuminated by the pale light filtering through the meetinghouse's plain glass windows, reflected the particular strain that had settled over Salem Village in recent months. Fear lived in their eyes—fear of Indian raids, fear of crop failures, fear of their neighbors, and increasingly, fear of the Devil himself.

"Let us pray," Matthias began, his voice carrying the authority that three years of ministerial service had cultivated, "for deliverance from the snares of Satan, and for the wisdom to discern truth from falsehood in these troubled times."

The words felt like ash in his mouth. Even as he spoke of discerning truth, Matthias carried within himself a secret that would brand him as the very evil he preached against. The power that lived in his mind—the ability to reach into another person's memories and reshape them like clay in a potter's hands—was precisely the sort of supernatural gift that the good people of Salem would burn him for possessing.

As the congregation bowed their heads in prayer, Matthias found his gaze drawn to Sarah Osborne, sitting in the back pew with her head tilted at an angle that suggested she was listening to something the rest of them could not hear. For weeks now, he had noticed odd behaviors from several villagers—moments when they seemed to see things that weren't there, instances of knowledge they shouldn't possess, healings that occurred too quickly to be natural.

Salem Village was harboring secrets. Some of them might be the very secrets his family had been sworn to protect for over three centuries.

The prayer concluded, and Matthias opened his Bible to the text he had selected for this morning's sermon. But as he began to read from Deuteronomy about the need to purge evil from among them, his attention was drawn to young Mercy Lewis, who sat rigidly in the second row, her eyes fixed on a point just above his head with an expression of growing terror.

Matthias followed her gaze and felt his blood chill. There, barely visible even to his enhanced senses, was a figure that should not exist—a shadow with substance, a darkness that moved with purpose and intelligence. He had read about such things in the family records hidden beneath his house, descriptions of supernatural entities that fed on fear and chaos.

As he watched, the shadow-thing descended toward the congregation, and Mercy Lewis began to convulse.

"The Devil!" she shrieked, pointing directly at the space where only Matthias could clearly see the entity. "He comes for us! He sends his familiars to torment the faithful!"

The meetinghouse erupted into chaos. Some congregants fled toward the doors while others surged forward to help the convulsing girl. Matthias found himself torn between his duty as a minister to bring order and his deeper knowledge that something genuinely supernatural was occurring in his church.

As Mercy's convulsions intensified, other girls began to show similar symptoms. Abigail Williams, the minister's niece from Salem Town who had been visiting for the week, fell to the floor screaming about invisible hands that clawed at her flesh. Mary Warren, a servant girl known for her practical nature, began speaking in a voice that was not her own—a voice that spoke in Latin phrases no village girl should know.

Matthias acted on instinct, stepping down from his pulpit and moving toward the afflicted girls. As he approached, he reached out with his supernatural senses and immediately understood what was happening. The shadow-entity was not a demon in the traditional sense, but something else—a creature drawn to communities where supernatural abilities lay dormant or suppressed, feeding on the psychic energy that built up when the gifted were forced to hide their true nature.

The girls were not possessed in any biblical sense. They were gifted, their abilities awakening under the stress of the entity's presence, manifesting in ways that appeared demonic to those who didn't understand the true nature of supernatural power.

"Stand back," Matthias commanded, his voice carrying an authority that went beyond his ministerial office. "Let me pray over them."

He knelt beside Mercy Lewis and placed his hand on her forehead, ostensibly to offer pastoral comfort. But what he actually did was far more complex. Reaching into her mind with his power, he found the memories of what she had truly seen—not the Devil, but a creature of shadow and hunger that existed in the spaces between worlds. With delicate precision, he began to reshape those memories, transforming the supernatural truth into something more conventionally explainable.

In the revised version of events he planted in her mind, Mercy had simply been overcome by religious fervor and the bitter cold. She had fainted during the particularly intense sermon, her mind creating hallucinatory visions as her body struggled with the physical stress. It was an explanation the Puritan community could accept—spiritual ecstasy was not uncommon during powerful preaching.

As Matthias worked on Mercy's memories, he became aware that the shadow-entity was watching him with something approaching curiosity. It had expected to feed on the growing supernatural chaos, but instead found its meal being systematically dismantled by someone who understood its nature. With what might have been the equivalent of a shrug, the creature faded back into whatever realm it had emerged from, seeking easier prey elsewhere.

One by one, Matthias moved through the afflicted girls, carefully editing their memories to remove any trace of genuine supernatural experience. Abigail Williams had been overcome by worry about her family's financial struggles. Mary Warren had been suffering from a fever that caused temporary delirium. Each explanation was mundane, believable, and completely false.

By the time the village doctor arrived, summoned by concerned parishioners, the crisis had passed. The girls were weak but coherent, able to describe their experiences in terms that fit within the accepted framework of Puritan theology and medicine. Dr. Griggs examined them thoroughly and pronounced that they had suffered from nothing more than religious hysteria combined with the effects of the harsh winter.

But as the congregation dispersed and the meetinghouse emptied, Matthias remained behind, trembling with the magnitude of what he had done. For the first time in his adult life, he had used his supernatural gift openly, if covertly. He had reached into human minds and reshaped their very memories, violating the most fundamental boundaries of individual will and consciousness.

The weight of that violation pressed down on him like a physical force. His Puritan faith taught that the soul was inviolate, that each person's relationship with God was sacred and individual. By altering memories, had he not committed a kind of spiritual rape? Had he not played God with the very essence of human experience?

But the alternative—allowing the girls to retain their memories of genuine supernatural events—would have been far worse. Salem Village was already a tinderbox of suspicion and fear. If word spread that actual supernatural entities were manifesting in the meetinghouse, it would trigger exactly the kind of exposure that his family had spent centuries preventing.

Matthias made his way home through the village streets, nodding to neighbors who offered words of praise for his handling of the morning's crisis. They saw him as a steady hand in troubled times, a minister who had prevented religious hysteria from spiraling out of control. If they only knew the truth of how he had accomplished that prevention...

The Ashford house sat on a small rise overlooking Salem Village, a modest but well-built structure that had housed three generations of his family since their arrival in the Massachusetts Bay Colony. As he entered through the front door, Matthias was greeted by his wife Ruth, whose worried expression told him that word of the morning's events had already reached her.

"Is it true?" she asked immediately. "Did the Devil manifest in the meetinghouse?"

"No," Matthias replied, which was technically accurate. "The girls suffered from hysteria brought on by the cold and the intensity of religious feeling. Dr. Griggs has confirmed it."

Ruth's relief was visible. As the minister's wife, she carried her own burden of maintaining their family's reputation and standing in the community. Any suggestion of supernatural events connected to her husband's ministry would have been catastrophic for their position.

"Thank God," she murmured. "Though I wonder... there have been so many strange reports lately. The Corey boy claiming to see his dead grandmother, Mary English swearing that her spinning wheel operates itself, old Joseph Putnam insisting that his animals speak to him in human voices."

Matthias felt his stomach clench. Each of the incidents Ruth described sounded like the awakening of supernatural gifts, the kind of abilities that had been surfacing with increasing frequency in communities where the gifted had intermarried for generations. Salem Village, with its history of settlement by families fleeing religious persecution in England, might well be home to descendants of Eleanor's original covenant.

"People see what they expect to see in troubled times," he said carefully. "Fear makes us interpret natural events as supernatural ones."

But even as he spoke the words, Matthias knew he would need to investigate further. If there were other gifted individuals in Salem Village, and if their abilities were beginning to manifest openly, the situation could spiral beyond his ability to control. He thought of the shadow-entity that had appeared in the meetinghouse, drawn by the supernatural energy of awakening gifts. How many more such creatures might be attracted to Salem if the gifted continued to emerge?

After Ruth retired for the evening, Matthias made his way to the cellar beneath their house, where behind a false wall lay the family archives that had been passed down from father to son since his ancestor William Ashford had joined Eleanor Blackthorne's covenant in 1349. The documents were wrapped in oiled leather and preserved with care that bordered on reverence—letters from other covenant families, reports of supernatural events that had been successfully suppressed, and most importantly, Eleanor's own journal describing the vision that had started it all.

Matthias lit a candle and spread the documents across his wooden desk, searching for guidance in the words of his predecessors. What he found was both reassuring and terrifying. The Ashford family had dealt with similar awakenings before—moments when the supernatural gifts inherited from covenant bloodlines had begun to surface in communities where multiple families had settled.

His grandfather had written about an incident in Connecticut in 1647, when several young people had begun manifesting abilities during a period of religious revival. The situation had been contained through careful memory manipulation and the strategic relocation of the most powerful gifted individuals. His great-grandfather had described a similar crisis in Boston in 1692, resolved through what he cryptically referred to as "selective editing of problematic recollections."

But the most relevant document was a letter from Eleanor herself, written shortly before her death in 1402 and addressed to future generations of the covenant. In it, she warned of periods when the supernatural would break through into the natural world despite all efforts at concealment, drawn by concentrations of gifted blood or moments of particular stress and upheaval.

"When such times come," Eleanor had written in her precise medieval script, *"remember that preservation of the secret must take precedence over all other considerations. Use whatever gifts you possess to maintain the illusion of normalcy, even if doing so requires actions that conflict with your personal beliefs or moral convictions. The alternative—exposure and the catastrophe that follows—is always worse than any individual violation of conscience."*

The words provided justification for what Matthias had done in the meetinghouse, but they did not ease the burden of guilt that pressed upon his soul. Eleanor's covenant demanded sacrifices that went beyond mere secrecy—it required its members to become active conspirators in the suppression of truth, to use their supernatural gifts against their own communities for the supposed greater good.

Matthias carefully returned the documents to their hiding place and made his way back upstairs, his mind churning with the implications of what he had learned. Salem Village was sitting on a supernatural powder keg, with gifted individuals beginning to manifest abilities they didn't understand and entities from beyond being drawn to the growing psychic disturbance.

As the minister responsible for the spiritual welfare of the community, he had the perfect position to monitor and control such manifestations. But doing so would require him to become something he had never intended to be—not just a keeper of family secrets, but an active agent of supernatural suppression.

The irony was not lost on him. He had been called to the ministry out of a genuine desire to serve God and help his fellow humans. Now he found himself in a position where serving God—as he understood the divine will through Eleanor's covenant—required him to manipulate and deceive those same fellow humans.

Outside his window, Salem Village slept peacefully under a blanket of February snow, unaware that their minister carried the power to reshape their very memories and the burden of deciding which truths they were allowed to know. Tomorrow would bring new challenges, new manifestations of the supernatural that would need to be carefully managed.

But tonight, Matthias Ashford knelt beside his bed and prayed—not for guidance in his ministerial duties, but for the strength to bear the weight of choices that no human being should have to make. In the darkness of his chamber, surrounded by the sleeping innocence of his community, he began to understand the true cost of Eleanor's covenant.

The gathering of the gifted had been difficult. The formal creation of their pact had been solemn. But living with the consequences, generation after generation, might be the hardest burden of all.

CHAPTER 7: THE TRUE WITCH

Salem Village, Massachusetts

March 1692

The examination chamber in Ingersoll's tavern was thick with the stench of unwashed bodies, fear, and something else that made Matthias's supernatural senses recoil—the metallic tang of genuine power being forcibly suppressed. He stood near the back of the crowded room, ostensibly present in his role as village minister to offer spiritual guidance during the proceedings, but in truth studying the accused woman who sat bound before the magistrates with an intensity that had nothing to do with pastoral concern.

Sarah Good was not what the crowd expected from a witch. Where folklore painted such women as ancient crones with wild hair and haunting eyes, Sarah was perhaps thirty years of age, with the calloused hands of someone who had worked hard all her life and the hollow-cheeked gauntness of someone who had known too much hunger. But it was her eyes that captured Matthias's attention—eyes that held a depth of understanding that spoke of gifts carefully hidden and power deliberately restrained.

Magistrate John Hathorne leaned forward in his chair, his voice carrying the authority of the Massachusetts Bay Colony's legal system. "Sarah Good, what evil spirit have you familiarity with?"

"None," Sarah replied, her voice steady despite the chains that bound her wrists. "I am falsely accused."

"Have you made no contract with the Devil?"

"No."

Hathorne gestured toward the front of the room, where the afflicted girls sat in a row like judges themselves. "Then explain why these children are tormented in your presence. Even now, look how they suffer."

Matthias watched as the girls—Mercy Lewis, Abigail Williams, and several others whose memories he had edited just weeks before—began their practiced performance of supernatural affliction. They writhed and cried out, claiming to see Sarah's specter tormenting them even as she sat chained and motionless. The performance was convincing enough to fool most observers, but Matthias could see the deliberate nature of their movements, the careful timing of their cries.

What concerned him more was what he sensed beneath the theatrical display. These girls were not simply playacting—they were channeling something real, drawing on genuine supernatural sensitivity that had been awakened and then misdirected. Someone had taught them to access their latent abilities and use them to create the appearance of demonic affliction.

"I do not torment them," Sarah said, her voice carrying a ring of absolute truth that only someone with Matthias's enhanced perceptions could fully appreciate. "I go along with my life. I am innocent of these charges."

As the examination continued, Matthias found himself studying not just Sarah but the entire proceedings with growing unease. The questions followed a pattern that seemed designed less to uncover truth than to create a specific narrative—one that would discredit any genuine supernatural activity by mixing it with obvious falsehoods and hysterical accusations.

It was then that he noticed the other observer, a man standing near the front of the room whose presence made Matthias's supernatural senses prickle with recognition. Tall and lean with graying hair and eyes that missed nothing, the stranger watched the proceedings with the detached interest of someone evaluating the success of a carefully orchestrated performance.

When their gazes met across the crowded room, Matthias felt the familiar shock of contact with another member of Eleanor's covenant. The man's slight nod confirmed what Matthias's senses had already told him—he was not the only descendant of the original conspiracy present in Salem.

The examination concluded with Sarah's commitment to Boston jail to await formal trial, her protestations of innocence ignored by magistrates who had already decided her guilt. As the crowd dispersed, Matthias made his way toward the stranger, who waited for him near the tavern's back entrance.

"Reverend Ashford," the man said quietly, his voice carrying the educated accent of someone from a higher social class than his simple clothes suggested. "I am Samuel Parris. Perhaps we might speak privately?"

Matthias felt a chill of recognition. Parris was the minister of Salem Village—his counterpart in Salem Town, and the uncle of Abigail Williams, one of the primary accusers. "Of course, Reverend Parris. Though I confess surprise at meeting you here rather than in your own parish."

Parris gestured toward a secluded corner of the tavern's common room, away from the lingering crowd. "My presence here is not in my capacity as a minister, but rather in service to older obligations. Obligations I believe you share."

The coded language was familiar to Matthias from his family's archives. For over three centuries, covenant members had developed ways of identifying and communicating with each other without revealing their nature to outsiders. Parris was confirming what Matthias had already suspected—that the Salem witch trials were not the natural outbreak of hysteria they appeared to be.

"What obligations are those?" Matthias asked carefully.

"The preservation of necessary secrets," Parris replied. "The maintenance of helpful illusions. The protection of humanity from truths it is not prepared to understand."

Matthias felt the pieces of a larger puzzle beginning to fall into place. "The accused women—are they...?"

"Some are gifted, yes. Others are simply convenient scapegoats to muddy the waters." Parris's expression was grim. "Sarah Good, whom you just observed, possesses genuine healing abilities. She has been using them quietly for years, helping women through difficult births, easing the suffering of the dying. But her discretion has been... insufficient."

"Someone noticed her abilities?"

"Several people. Recoveries that were too rapid, interventions that were too successful, patterns that raised questions among those observant enough to see them." Parris paused, watching as the last of the crowd filtered out of the tavern. "The situation required management."

Matthias felt his stomach clench with understanding. "You orchestrated her accusation."

"I orchestrated a controlled revelation," Parris corrected. "Better to have Sarah's abilities exposed in a context where they will be dismissed as demonic deception than to allow them to be recognized for what they truly are. The witch trials serve a dual purpose—they allow us to identify and manage gifted individuals while simultaneously discrediting the very concept of supernatural abilities."

The casual way Parris discussed the manipulation of lives and the orchestration of what would likely be capital trials made Matthias's blood run cold. "And the other accused? Bridget Bishop, Rebecca Nurse, the others?"

"A mixture. Some, like Rebecca Nurse, are genuinely innocent—their accusations serve to dilute the credibility of the proceedings. Others possess minor gifts that have attracted unwanted attention. A few, like Bridget Bishop, have been using their abilities too openly and needed to be... discouraged."

Matthias thought of Sarah Good, sitting in chains in Boston jail, facing execution for the crime of using her gifts to help others. "This is not what Eleanor intended when she founded the covenant."

"Isn't it?" Parris's voice carried a challenge. "Read her final letters, Ashford. Read what she wrote about the necessity of whatever measures might be required to preserve the secret. The covenant has been orchestrating witch trials for over two centuries—in Germany, in Scotland, in England. Always for the same purpose: to create a framework where genuine supernatural activity can be dismissed as hysteria or demonic deception."

The revelation hit Matthias like a physical blow. He had always understood that the covenant required secrecy and sacrifice, but he had never imagined that it might actively participate in the persecution of the very people it was meant to protect. The moral implications were staggering.

"How many?" he asked quietly.

"How many what?"

"How many gifted individuals have been executed because of covenant orchestration?"

Parris was quiet for a long moment. "Fewer than would have died if their abilities had been recognized for what they truly were. Sometimes individual sacrifices are necessary to preserve the larger secret."

Matthias felt his world tilting on its axis. Everything he had believed about his family's noble mission, about the covenant's role as protector of the gifted, was being recontextualized in terms of calculated betrayal and systematic murder.

"The girls," he said suddenly. "The afflicted children. They have genuine sensitivity, don't they? You've awakened their gifts and taught them to use them for this deception."

"Some of them, yes. Mercy Lewis has prophetic abilities that rival those of Eleanor herself. Abigail Williams can sense the presence of supernatural power in others. We have... guided their development in ways that serve our purposes."

"You've turned children into weapons against their own kind."

"We've given them a purpose that protects the covenant while satisfying their need to use their abilities." Parris's tone was matter-of-fact, as if discussing the management of livestock rather than the corruption of young lives. "It's more humane than forcing them to suppress their gifts entirely."

Matthias stared at this man who shared his covenant heritage but seemed to possess none of the moral qualms that tormented Matthias's own conscience. "And Sarah Good? What happens to her now?"

"That depends on you," Parris replied. "Your memory manipulation abilities could be useful in managing her case. We could alter the recollections of key witnesses, create inconsistencies in testimony that would lead to her acquittal. Or we could allow the proceedings to follow their natural course."

"You mean we could let her hang for the crime of helping people."

"We could allow her to become a martyr whose death serves to reinforce the narrative that supernatural abilities are demonic in nature, thereby protecting hundreds of other gifted individuals who remain hidden." Parris leaned closer, his voice dropping to barely above a whisper. "Choose carefully, Ashford. Your decision here will determine whether you're truly committed to the covenant's mission or merely playing at being one of us."

Matthias felt the weight of an impossible choice settling on his shoulders. Save Sarah Good and risk exposing himself and other covenant members, or allow an innocent woman to die to preserve a system that had apparently been murdering the gifted for centuries.

Before he could respond, the tavern door opened and a young woman entered, moving with the careful gait of someone trying not to attract attention. Matthias's supernatural senses immediately identified her as gifted—her presence carried the same golden thread quality he had learned to recognize in others like himself.

The woman approached their corner table with obvious nervousness, her eyes darting around the room to ensure they weren't being observed. "Reverend Parris," she whispered, "I've been watching the jail as you instructed. Sarah's condition is worsening. The chains they've put her in are somehow interfering with her ability to access her gift. She's growing weaker."

Parris nodded grimly. "Iron has that effect on some of the gifted. An unfortunate complication, but not an unexpected one."

"Then you have to help her," the woman said urgently. "If she dies in jail before the trial—"

"Then the problem resolves itself," Parris interrupted coldly. "A death from natural causes while in custody serves our purposes just as well as a formal execution."

The casual way he discussed Sarah's potential death galvanized Matthias into action. Whatever the risks, whatever the consequences for the covenant's larger mission, he could not stand by and watch an innocent woman die for the crime of helping others.

"No," he said firmly. "I won't be party to murder, direct or indirect."

Parris studied him with the cold calculation of a chess player evaluating an opponent's move. "Then you'll intervene?"

"I'll do what I can to save her without exposing the covenant. But I won't participate in this... this systematic betrayal of everything Eleanor's mission was supposed to represent."

"Eleanor's mission," Parris said quietly, "was to prevent the extinction of humanity. Everything else—including the lives of individual gifted persons—is secondary to that goal."

But Matthias was no longer listening. His mind was already working through the possibilities, the ways he might use his memory manipulation abilities to save Sarah without triggering the larger exposure that Parris warned against. It would be dangerous, perhaps impossible, but the alternative—complicity in a system that murdered the innocent to preserve its own secrets—was unthinkable.

As he rose from the table, Matthias caught sight of his reflection in the tavern's window glass. The face that looked back at him was that of a man who had discovered that his life's purpose was built on a foundation of lies and systematic betrayal. The covenant he had been raised to serve was not the noble protector of the gifted he had believed it to be, but something far darker—a conspiracy that preserved itself by sacrificing its own members whenever convenience demanded.

"I'll save her," he said to Parris, his voice carrying a conviction that surprised him with its strength. "Whatever the cost."

Parris nodded slowly, as if he had expected this response. "Then you'd better move quickly. The trial is scheduled for next week, and iron poisoning works faster than most people realize."

As Matthias left the tavern and made his way through Salem's darkening streets, he found himself thinking not of Eleanor's original vision, but of the choice that every generation of the covenant seemed destined to face: whether to preserve the organization's secrets or protect the innocent people those secrets were supposed to serve.

For the first time since learning of his heritage, Matthias wondered if Eleanor's vision had been wrong—not about the danger of revealing supernatural abilities, but about the methods required to prevent that revelation. Perhaps the covenant had become the very thing it had been created to fight against: a force that destroyed the gifted in the name of protecting them.

The thought was heretical, dangerous, potentially catastrophic for everything his family had worked for across the centuries. But as he prepared to risk everything to save one innocent woman, Matthias found himself wondering if heresy might sometimes be another word for conscience.

CHAPTER 8: MEMORY THIEF

Salem Village, Massachusetts

April 1692

The first time Matthias deliberately violated another person's mind, he vomited afterward for nearly an hour.

It had been necessary—John Proctor had witnessed Mary Warren levitating three feet above her bed during what appeared to be a fit of supernatural possession, and Proctor was a man of sufficient standing in the community that his testimony could not simply be dismissed. So Matthias had visited the Proctor farm under the pretense of offering pastoral comfort, and while John's wife Elizabeth served them cider, he had carefully reached into John's memories and reshaped them.

The process was more invasive than anything Matthias had done before. Where his earlier interventions with the afflicted girls had been surface manipulations—adjusting interpretations of events rather than fundamental recollections—this required him to dig deep into John's consciousness and extract a specific memory like a tumor from healthy flesh.

He found the moment easily enough: John standing in his doorway, watching in horrified fascination as his servant girl floated in midair, her eyes rolled back and her voice speaking in languages that had been dead for centuries. The memory was vivid, clear, impossible to dismiss as imagination or hysteria.

Matthias wrapped his supernatural gift around that memory like surgical instruments around a growth and began the delicate work of extraction. He preserved the emotional context—John's concern for Mary, his desire to help—but replaced the impossible image of levitation with something more mundane: Mary thrashing on the bed in the grip of a fever-induced seizure, her movements so violent that she seemed to bounce and rise from the mattress.

The revision was seamless, consistent with John's other memories of the event, and completely false.

Afterward, as Matthias stumbled away from the Proctor farm and into the woods beyond, his body rebelled against what his mind had done. The violation of another person's consciousness, the theft of truth from someone who trusted him, the casual rewriting of reality itself—it was too much for his Puritan-raised conscience to bear.

But it was only the beginning.

Over the following weeks, as the witch trials gained momentum and genuine supernatural events multiplied throughout Salem, Matthias found himself making increasingly frequent pastoral visits to witnesses whose memories required... adjustment. There was Giles Corey, who had seen his wife Martha healing a neighbor's broken arm with nothing more than a touch and a whispered prayer. There was Susannah Martin, who had been observed walking across Newbury Harbor at low tide without sinking into the mud—an impossible feat that required extensive revision to transform into a simple crossing at an unusually solid section of the shoreline.

Each intervention was a violation, and each violation left its mark on Matthias's soul.

The worst part was how good he was becoming at it. What had initially required hours of careful mental surgery could now be accomplished in minutes. He learned to identify the specific neural pathways where memories were stored, to distinguish between core recollections and peripheral details, to edit experiences so skillfully that the subjects never suspected their minds had been invaded.

He was becoming exactly what his Puritan theology warned against: a servant of the Father of Lies, someone who dealt in deception and false witness. But every time his conscience threatened to overwhelm his resolve, Matthias reminded himself of the alternative. Without his interventions, Salem would already have erupted into the very supernatural revelation that Eleanor's covenant existed to prevent.

"You've been having nightmares," Ruth observed one morning as she prepared breakfast in their kitchen. Her voice carried the careful neutrality of someone who had been watching her husband with growing concern for weeks.

Matthias looked up from the sermon notes he had been pretending to review. "Have I? I hadn't noticed."

"Every night for the past month. You talk in your sleep—fragments of things that don't make sense. Names of people I don't recognize, conversations about memories and forgetting." Ruth set a bowl of porridge before him with the deliberate precision of someone trying to maintain normalcy in the face of the inexplicable. "Sometimes you weep."

The observation hit Matthias like a physical blow. He had thought his growing guilt was contained, confined to his waking hours when he could at least attempt to maintain the facade of ministerial composure. The idea that his unconscious mind was betraying the weight of his actions was terrifying.

"The trials have been... difficult," he said carefully. "Witnessing the community's suffering, trying to provide comfort in such dark times. Perhaps the strain is affecting my rest."

Ruth sat across from him at their simple wooden table, her hands folded in her lap in the manner she adopted when preparing to say something important. "Matthias, I've been your wife for seven years. I know when you're keeping secrets from me."

The directness of her statement made Matthias's blood run cold. Ruth was an intelligent woman, observant and intuitive in ways that had initially attracted him to her. Those same qualities now made her potentially dangerous to the secrets he carried.

"What secrets could I possibly keep from you?" he asked, forcing lightness into his voice.

"I don't know. That's what worries me." Ruth reached across the table and took his hand, her touch warm and familiar. "You've changed since the trials began. You're distant, distracted. You disappear for hours on pastoral visits that should take minutes. And when you return..." She paused, studying his face with eyes that seemed to see too much. "When you return, you look like a man who's done something he can never forgive himself for."

Matthias felt the familiar temptation to reach out with his gift, to smooth away Ruth's suspicions as easily as he had edited the memories of John Proctor and the others. It would be simple—a minor adjustment to her recollections of his recent behavior, a subtle dampening of her observational instincts regarding his activities. She would never know the difference.

The fact that he was even considering such an action horrified him more than all his previous violations combined. Ruth wasn't a witness to supernatural events that threatened the covenant's secrecy. She was his wife, the woman he loved, someone whose trust and respect formed the foundation of his identity as a man. The thought of manipulating her memories represented a line he had never imagined he might cross.

"The trials are demanding," he said finally, the words feeling inadequate and false in his mouth. "Perhaps when they conclude, things will return to normal."

Ruth studied his face for a long moment, clearly recognizing the deflection for what it was. But instead of pressing further, she simply squeezed his hand and nodded. "I pray that's true. Whatever burden you're carrying, husband, remember that God's grace is sufficient for all sins. Even those we think ourselves incapable of committing."

Her words followed Matthias throughout the day as he made his rounds through Salem Village, checking on parishioners and gathering intelligence about any new supernatural manifestations that might require his intervention. The irony of Ruth's theological comfort was not lost on him—she spoke of God's grace for sins, unaware that her husband's sins involved the systematic violation of divine gifts that God himself had presumably granted to the afflicted.

That evening, seeking guidance or perhaps just comfort from his family's history, Matthias descended once again to the hidden chamber beneath his house. But this time, instead of reaching for the familiar documents he had studied countless times before, he found himself drawn to a section of the archives he had never fully explored—a collection of letters and journals from covenant members in the centuries following Eleanor's death.

What he found there shattered any remaining illusions about the noble nature of his family's mission.

The documents revealed a pattern that stretched back over three hundred years: systematic betrayals, orchestrated persecutions, and the calculated sacrifice of gifted individuals whenever their existence threatened the covenant's secrecy. A letter from Germany in 1487 described the covenant's role in identifying and eliminating a group of healers whose successes had attracted the attention of local authorities. A journal from Scotland in 1563 detailed the deliberate provocation of witch trials to discredit reports of genuine supernatural activity.

Most damning of all was a series of correspondence between covenant leaders in the 1640s, discussing what they referred to as "the French Solution"—the strategic placement of covenant members in positions of authority within the Catholic Church's Inquisition, allowing them to direct persecution away from fellow covenant members and toward individuals whose gifts posed a threat to secrecy.

Matthias read with growing horror as the letters described the torture and execution of dozens of genuinely gifted individuals, their deaths justified as necessary sacrifices to preserve the larger secret. One letter, written by someone identified only as "E.B." (possibly one of Eleanor's descendants), laid out the philosophical framework that justified such actions:

"We must never forget that our covenant exists not to protect the gifted, but to protect humanity from the consequences of supernatural revelation. Individual members of our kind are expendable if their sacrifice serves the greater mission. Eleanor herself recognized this truth in her final years, acknowledging that

109

the preservation of secrecy might sometimes require the elimination of those who threaten it."

The documents went on to describe the development of what they called "controlled revelations"—situations where the covenant would deliberately expose certain gifted individuals in contexts designed to discredit the very concept of supernatural abilities. The Salem witch trials, Matthias realized with mounting dread, were simply the latest iteration of a strategy that had been refined over centuries of practice.

As he read deeper into the archives, Matthias discovered references to techniques he had never encountered in his family's training materials—methods for identifying gifted individuals who were unaware of their own abilities, protocols for eliminating covenant members who showed signs of rebellion against the organization's methods, and most chilling of all, procedures for what they termed "selective memory architecture" in the descendants of covenant families.

This last reference led him to a collection of documents that made his blood run cold. For generations, the covenant had been systematically editing the memories of its own children, ensuring that each new generation received only the information deemed necessary for their assigned role within the organization. Matthias himself, he realized with dawning horror, might be carrying memories that had been carefully curated by his predecessors.

The possibility that his own recollections of childhood, of his father's teachings about the covenant, of the very foundations of his understanding about their mission, might be carefully constructed lies was almost too much to bear. How could he trust any of his memories if the organization he served had made a practice of editing the minds of its own members?

A noise from upstairs interrupted his increasingly frantic research—Ruth moving about the house, preparing for bed. Matthias carefully returned the documents to their hiding places, but his mind continued to churn with the implications of what he had discovered.

Everything he thought he knew about Eleanor's covenant was potentially false. The noble mission of protecting the gifted from persecution had apparently been perverted into a system that actively participated in that persecution. The organization that claimed to preserve supernatural abilities for the future was systematically eliminating anyone whose gifts might threaten their control.

And he—Matthias Ashford, minister of God, supposed protector of the innocent—had become a willing participant in this centuries-old conspiracy of betrayal and murder.

As he climbed the stairs to his bedroom, where Ruth waited with the trust and love of someone who still believed her husband to be the man she had married, Matthias found himself facing a choice that would define the rest of his life. He could continue serving the covenant, using his abilities to edit memories and suppress supernatural manifestations in service to an organization that apparently viewed him as just another expendable asset. Or he could find some way to resist, to protect the innocent people of Salem from both the supernatural chaos that threatened to engulf them and the covenant's systematic betrayal of its own principles.

The choice was complicated by a terrible uncertainty: if his own memories had been edited, could he even trust his moral instincts? How could he know what was right if he couldn't be certain what was real?

But as he looked at Ruth's sleeping face in the moonlight that filtered through their bedroom window, one thing became clear. Whatever else might be false in his life, whatever lies might have been planted in his memories, his love for his wife was real. The guilt that tore at his conscience when he violated other people's minds was real. The horror he felt at discovering the covenant's true nature was real.

And if those feelings were real, then perhaps they could serve as a compass to guide him through the moral darkness that had engulfed his life.

Tomorrow would bring new challenges, new supernatural manifestations that would require management, new memories that might need to be edited to preserve the covenant's secrets. But tonight, Matthias Ashford made a decision that would echo through the generations of his family that followed.

He would find a way to be more than just a memory thief in service to an organization that had lost its way. He would find a way to protect the innocent, even if it meant betraying everything he had been raised to believe about his duty to Eleanor's covenant.

The decision felt like stepping off a cliff into darkness. But for the first time in months, it also felt like something that might, eventually, lead to redemption.

CHAPTER 9: THE PRICE OF PROTECTION

Salem Village, Massachusetts

May 1692

Matthias stood in the doorway of Rebecca Nurse's cell, watching the elderly woman sleep fitfully on the straw-covered floor of Salem jail. Even in the dim light filtering through the barred window, he could see the golden aura that marked her as one of the gifted—a gentle, healing presence that had made her beloved in the community for decades. Now that same gift had made her a target of accusations that would likely see her hanged before summer's end.

"She doesn't even know what she is," whispered Mary Esty, Rebecca's sister, who sat in the adjacent cell. "All her life, people have recovered faster when she tends them, children have calmed at her touch, but she's always attributed it to God's grace working through her prayers."

Matthias nodded grimly. In the past month, he had identified nearly a dozen genuinely gifted individuals among the accused—people whose abilities had manifested so subtly, so gradually, that they themselves remained unaware of their supernatural nature. The covenant's systematic persecution was not just targeting the obviously powerful, but anyone whose bloodline carried even the faintest trace of Eleanor's legacy.

"I can help her," he said quietly, though the words tasted like ash in his mouth. "Alter the memories of the key witnesses, create inconsistencies in the testimony that will lead to acquittal."

"And the cost?" Mary's eyes were sharp despite her own imprisonment. She was gifted too, though more aware of her abilities than her sister—a woman who could sense the presence of supernatural power in others, which had made her useful to the covenant until she had begun asking too many questions about the trials' true purpose.

Matthias didn't answer immediately. The cost was something he was only beginning to understand. Each time he reached into another person's mind, each memory he edited or erased, it became easier to blur the lines of his own consciousness. Increasingly, he found himself uncertain which thoughts were his own and which were borrowed from the minds he had violated. Sometimes he would start to remember events from the perspective of people whose memories he had altered, as if their revised experiences were somehow contaminating his own recollections.

"The cost is mine to pay," he said finally.

"Is it?" Mary leaned forward, her voice dropping to barely above a whisper. "How many minds have you touched, Matthias? How many memories have you rewritten? And how certain are you that your own thoughts remain untainted by the process?"

The question hit closer to home than Mary could have known. Just that morning, Matthias had found himself remembering a conversation with Samuel Parris that he was almost certain had never taken place—or had it? The more he used his gift, the more his own memories seemed to shift and blur, as if the act of manipulating other minds was somehow destabilizing his own consciousness.

A sound from the corridor outside interrupted their conversation—footsteps approaching with the measured cadence of someone who belonged in this place of imprisonment and despair. Matthias turned to see Samuel Parris himself, accompanied by a tall, severe-looking man that Matthias didn't recognize.

"Reverend Ashford," Parris said with the false warmth he had perfected for public occasions. "How fortuitous to find you here. May I present Reverend Jonathan Blackthorne, recently arrived from Connecticut to assist with the trials."

The name sent a chill through Matthias's soul. Blackthorne—a descendant of Eleanor herself, carrying the most prestigious bloodline in the covenant's hierarchy. The man's presence here could only mean that Matthias's recent activities had attracted attention from the highest levels of the organization.

Blackthorne studied Matthias with eyes that seemed to see too much. "I've been reviewing the trial records, Reverend Ashford. Interesting patterns emerging in the witness testimonies—inconsistencies, memory lapses, sudden reversals of previously certain recollections. Almost as if someone has been... editing the proceedings."

"The strain of the trials affects everyone," Matthias replied carefully. "People sometimes remember events differently under pressure."

"Indeed they do." Blackthorne's smile was cold as winter iron. "Particularly when they receive assistance in their recollections. Walk with me, Reverend. There are matters we need to discuss privately."

They left the jail and made their way to Salem's church, where Blackthorne had apparently established a temporary office in the vestry. The space was dominated by a large table covered with documents—not just trial records, but maps, genealogical charts, and what appeared to be detailed profiles of every accused individual in the current proceedings.

"The Salem trials represent a masterpiece of covenant planning," Blackthorne began without preamble. "Three years in the making, coordinated between multiple families, designed to accomplish several objectives simultaneously. The elimination of problematic gifted individuals who had become too visible. The discrediting of supernatural phenomena through association with obvious fraud. The identification and recruitment of promising young sensitives. And most importantly..." He paused, fixing Matthias with a stare that seemed to pierce straight through to his soul. "The testing of covenant members to ensure their continued loyalty to our mission."

"Testing?" Matthias felt his blood run cold.

"Your recent activities have been instructive, Reverend Ashford. Your growing resistance to necessary measures, your unauthorized interventions on behalf of the accused, your increasing instability as documented in the reports of other covenant members." Blackthorne gestured to a thick file on the table. "All of it carefully noted and evaluated."

Matthias realized with dawning horror that he had been under surveillance, his every action monitored and analyzed by people he had trusted. "Reports from whom?"

"Your wife has been most helpful," Parris said from the doorway where he had positioned himself to block any attempt at escape. "Ruth Ashford, née Williams. Did you think we would allow a covenant member of your importance to marry outside our bloodlines without ensuring appropriate... monitoring?"

The betrayal hit Matthias like a physical blow. Ruth—his beloved wife, the one person he had thought remained pure and untainted by the covenant's machinations—had been reporting on him all along. Their marriage itself was apparently just another aspect of the organization's comprehensive control over his life.

"Seven years of marriage," Blackthorne continued conversationally, "seven years of detailed reports about your psychological state, your adherence to covenant principles, your potential for rebellion against organizational goals. Ruth has been quite thorough in her observations."

"She loves me," Matthias said weakly, though even as he spoke the words, he felt their inadequacy in the face of this revelation.

"I'm sure she does," Blackthorne agreed. "Love and duty are not mutually exclusive. Ruth understands that the covenant's mission transcends individual relationships. She also understands the consequences of failure to fulfill her obligations."

The threat implicit in those words was clear. Ruth's safety depended on her continued cooperation with the covenant's monitoring of Matthias. His wife was not just a spy—she was also a hostage to ensure his compliance.

"What do you want from me?" Matthias asked.

"Complete recommitment to the covenant's goals," Blackthorne replied. "Beginning with the elimination of the remaining problematic gifted individuals currently imprisoned here. Rebecca Nurse, Mary Esty, Martha Corey—all of them represent security threats that can no longer be tolerated."

"You want me to let them die."

"I want you to ensure they die," Blackthorne corrected. "Use your abilities to strengthen the case against them. Plant memories of supernatural activities in the minds of key witnesses. Create evidence that will guarantee their conviction and execution."

Matthias felt the last vestiges of his moral certainty crumbling away. "And if I refuse?"

"Then you join them," Parris said simply. "Your own trial has already been prepared, should it become necessary. Witnesses ready to testify about your unusual knowledge of the accused, your strange ability to calm the afflicted, your possession of books and documents that could be interpreted as evidence of diabolic studies."

"The covenant protects its own," Matthias said, though the words sounded hollow even to his own ears.

"The covenant protects those who serve its interests," Blackthorne replied. "Those who threaten the mission, regardless of their bloodline or previous service, become expendable. Surely your study of our history has shown you examples of this principle in action."

It had, of course. The documents in Matthias's family archives were filled with references to covenant members who had been eliminated when they posed threats to organizational security. He had always assumed those cases involved clear betrayals or gross incompetence. He had never imagined that simple moral qualms about the organization's methods could be grounds for execution.

"I need time to consider," Matthias said.

"Time is a luxury we cannot afford," Blackthorne replied. "The trials are accelerating. Public attention is beginning to focus too closely on the supernatural elements of the proceedings. We need resolution—complete resolution—within the week."

"And if the true nature of the trials is exposed?"

Blackthorne's expression darkened. "Then we implement the final protocol."

"Which is?"

"The elimination of Salem Village itself," Parris said quietly. "A tragic fire, perhaps. Or a particularly virulent outbreak of smallpox. Something that would kill all witnesses and destroy all evidence of what has occurred here."

The casual way they discussed the potential murder of an entire community—hundreds of innocent people whose only crime was living too close to the covenant's machinations—struck Matthias speechless. These men were not guardians of humanity but something far worse: a cancer that had grown within the very organization meant to protect the gifted.

"Choose quickly, Matthias," Blackthorne said, gathering his documents from the table. "Your decision will determine not just your own fate, but the fate of everyone you claim to care about. Including your beloved wife."

After they left, Matthias remained alone in the vestry, surrounded by the trappings of a faith that had once provided him with moral certainty but now seemed as hollow and manipulated as everything else in his life. The covenant he had been raised to serve had revealed itself to be a monstrous perversion of Eleanor's original vision—an organization that murdered the gifted to protect its own power and was willing to destroy entire communities to maintain its secrets.

But what choice did he have? If he refused to cooperate, Ruth would die along with him. If he complied, innocent people would hang while a system of systematic betrayal continued to spread its poison through future generations. And if he tried to expose the truth, Salem Village itself would be eliminated to prevent the revelation.

As the evening shadows lengthened through the church windows, Matthias made his decision. It was not the choice Blackthorne expected, nor the one that would ensure his own survival or Ruth's safety. But it was the only choice that offered any hope of redemption for the corruption that had infected Eleanor's covenant.

He would save as many of the gifted as possible, even at the cost of his own life. He would document the truth about the covenant's betrayal and ensure that future generations would understand what the organization had become. And he would find a way to protect Ruth from the consequences of his choice, even if it meant sacrificing everything else he had ever cared about.

The decision felt like stepping into an abyss, but for the first time in months, Matthias's conscience was clear. He had spent too long serving masters who demanded the violation of everything he held sacred. Now, at last, he would serve something higher than the covenant's corrupted version of Eleanor's vision.

He would serve the truth, whatever the cost.

Outside, Salem Village slept peacefully under the spring stars, unaware that its fate hung in the balance of one man's struggle between loyalty and conscience. Tomorrow would bring the final test of whether the covenant's corruption could be resisted or whether its cancer had spread too far to be stopped.

But tonight, Matthias Ashford prepared to become something the covenant had never expected one of its members to be: a genuine protector of the innocent, even against the organization that had created him.

CHAPTER 10: INVISIBLE SINS

Berlin, Germany

November 1943

Greta Müller stood invisible in the shadows of the Wannsee villa, watching SS-Oberführer Franz Konrad discuss the "relocation" of Berlin's remaining Jewish population with the cold efficiency of a man organizing a factory shift change. Through the window of his study, she could see the lake beyond, its dark waters reflecting the skeletal branches of winter trees like accusations against the gray November sky.

She had been invisible for three hours now, maintaining the supernatural gift that had made her invaluable to the Berlin resistance cell led by her brother Klaus. The ability to walk unseen through Nazi strongholds, to overhear conversations that could save lives, to gather intelligence that helped people escape the machinery of genocide—it was a power that had already preserved dozens of families from the transports heading east.

But it was also a power that came with a price her resistance comrades could never understand.

"The final sweep of the Rosenthaler district will commence Thursday morning," Konrad was saying to his aide, a young Untersturmführer whose eagerness to please made Greta's stomach turn. "Ensure the trucks are prepared for maximum capacity. The Reich's patience for delays has expired."

Greta closed her eyes, fighting the familiar wave of nausea that accompanied her espionage work. She knew what "maximum capacity" meant, just as she knew where those trucks would take their human cargo. The transit camp at Westerbork was merely a waystation. The real destinations were places like Auschwitz and Treblinka, names that had become synonymous with a horror so vast that the human mind struggled to comprehend it.

"What of the reports about unusual activities in the camps?" the aide asked. "Some of the guards have filed concerning observations about prisoners who seem to... survive impossible conditions."

Konrad's expression darkened. "Superstitious nonsense. The Führer has made his position clear—we deal in scientific reality, not folklore. If prisoners are surviving longer than anticipated, it merely indicates inefficiencies in the process that must be corrected."

But Greta heard something else in Konrad's tone, a note of unease that suggested he had received reports that couldn't be easily dismissed. Her supernatural senses, heightened by years of careful training, detected the tension that accompanied discussions of the inexplicable. Somewhere in the Nazi death machine, others like her were using their gifts to survive the unsurviable.

The knowledge filled her with a mixture of hope and despair. Hope that the gifted might find ways to endure even the worst humanity could devise. Despair that she was doing nothing to help them beyond her small contributions to the resistance's rescue efforts.

As Konrad continued his planning, Greta found herself remembering her grandmother's stories about the family's hidden heritage. Elsa Müller had been one of the last direct links to the original covenant families, her bloodline traceable back to a French weather-worker who had joined Eleanor Blackthorne's circle in 1349. The old woman had spent Greta's childhood filling her head with tales of secret gifts and sacred obligations, of a conspiracy of the supernatural that existed to protect humanity from its own fear.

"Never reveal what you are," Grandmother Elsa had whispered during long winter evenings when the family gathered around their fireplace. "Never use your gift where others might see. The world is not ready for what we carry, and it may never be. Better to let ordinary people suffer from ordinary causes than to risk the greater catastrophe that comes from revelation."

But what did those teachings mean when the suffering was anything but ordinary? When the causes were not natural disasters or random cruelties, but systematic, mechanized evil that turned human beings into numbers on efficiency reports?

Greta opened her eyes and forced herself to focus on Konrad's words, committing every detail to memory for her brother's resistance cell. But even as she gathered intelligence that might save a few more lives, she felt the weight of all the lives she could save if she abandoned her grandmother's teachings and used her gift openly.

She could walk invisible into the transit camps and unlock doors. She could render entire transport trains invisible until they reached safety. She could make guard towers vanish from sight, allowing thousands to escape while their captors stared in confusion at empty air. The scope of what her gift could accomplish, if used without restraint, was staggering.

But it was also exactly what the covenant existed to prevent.

The meeting concluded with handshakes and Heil Hitlers that made Greta's skin crawl. As Konrad and his aide departed, she remained motionless in the study, still invisible, struggling with the eternal dilemma that plagued every member of her hidden bloodline: How many people must suffer so that humanity itself might survive?

The sound of footsteps in the hallway alerted her to someone else's approach. Greta pressed herself against the wall, preparing to slip past whoever entered, but stopped when she sensed something impossible: another presence like her own, another golden thread in the fabric of ordinary reality.

The man who entered the study was tall and lean, with the bearing of a military officer despite his civilian clothes. His hair was dark with premature streaks of gray, and his eyes held the particular depth that came from seeing too much of human nature's worst impulses. But it was the aura around him that made Greta's breath catch—the unmistakable signature of supernatural power carefully contained.

He moved through the room with purpose, going directly to Konrad's desk and beginning to search through the papers with practiced efficiency. As he worked, Greta noticed something that made her supernatural senses scream in alarm: bullets holes in the wall behind him, and blood on his shirt, yet he showed no signs of injury or distress.

The man was gifted, and recently wounded, but somehow still functional.

Against every instinct for self-preservation that her grandmother had drilled into her, Greta allowed her invisibility to fade just enough to become a faint outline in the dim light of the study.

The man's head snapped up immediately, his hand moving to a concealed weapon with inhuman speed. But when he saw her semi-transparent form, his expression shifted from alarm to something approaching wonder.

"Mein Gott," he whispered in accented German. "Another one."

Greta solidified completely, stepping away from the wall with her hands visible and empty. "You're not German," she observed, noting the subtle markers in his pronunciation that suggested Eastern European origins.

"Soviet Union," he confirmed, though he didn't lower his guard. "Anton Volkov, currently operating under the identity of Heinrich Weber, architectural consultant." His smile was grim. "And you are someone who should not exist, according to everything I was taught as a child."

"Greta Müller. And I could say the same about you." She gestured toward the blood on his shirt. "How are you still standing?"

Anton glanced down at the stains, then began unbuttoning his shirt to reveal unmarked skin beneath. "Family gift, you might say. I heal quickly. Very quickly. What I cannot understand is how you managed to remain unseen while I searched this room. I was certain I was alone."

"Different gift." Greta allowed herself to fade slightly, becoming translucent again before returning to full visibility. "Invisibility. Useful for resistance work, though it comes with... complications."

"Complications?" Anton resumed his search of Konrad's desk, but kept his attention on Greta as he worked.

"Moral ones." The admission slipped out before Greta could stop it, surprising her with its honesty. "When you can walk unseen through places like this, when you witness what I've witnessed, the temptation to do more than just gather intelligence becomes overwhelming."

Anton's hands stilled on the papers he was examining. "You've seen the camps."

"Not directly. But I've heard enough planning sessions, read enough reports, seen enough transport lists to understand what's happening." Greta felt the familiar weight of helplessness settling on her shoulders. "Hundreds of thousands of people being systematically murdered, and I gather intelligence for a resistance cell that can save perhaps dozens at a time."

"And if you used your gift more openly?"

"I could save thousands," Greta said quietly. "But at the cost of revealing that people like us exist. And according to my family's teachings, that revelation would ultimately doom far more than I could ever save."

Anton closed his eyes for a moment, and Greta sensed a recognition in him that went beyond their shared supernatural nature. This was someone who had wrestled with the same impossible choices, who carried the same burden of inherited obligation to remain hidden while the world burned around them.

"Your family taught you about the old covenant," he said. It wasn't a question.

"Eleanor Blackthorne's conspiracy of shadows. The sacred duty to protect humanity from the consequences of supernatural revelation." Greta moved to the window, looking out at the lake where swans had once gathered before the war had driven even the wildlife into hiding. "My grandmother filled my childhood with stories about the need for secrecy, the catastrophic future that awaits if our gifts become known."

"Mine told similar stories," Anton said, returning to his search. "Though the version I learned emphasized the military applications of supernatural abilities. What happens when governments discover they can create soldiers who cannot be killed, spies who cannot be detected, weapons that transcend the limitations of ordinary matter."

"Yet here we are," Greta observed, "using our gifts in service to warring sides of the very conflict we're supposedly meant to avoid influencing."

"Here we are," Anton agreed, pulling a folder from the desk's bottom drawer. "Though I suspect our respective handlers have no idea what we truly are. They think I'm simply a very lucky soldier. You're probably seen as an extraordinarily skilled infiltrator."

"Something like that." Greta watched Anton photograph the documents he had found, noting the professional efficiency of his movements. "What did you find?"

"Transport schedules. Guard rotations. Something called Operation Bernhard—financial documents related to currency counterfeiting." Anton's expression darkened as he read. "And a memorandum about 'special prisoners' being held for Heinrich Himmler's personal inspection."

The last item made Greta's blood run cold. Himmler's fascination with the occult was well-documented among resistance circles, but the idea that he might have identified genuine supernatural individuals for study was terrifying.

"Special prisoners?"

"Children, mostly. Ages eight to sixteen, all demonstrating what the reports call 'statistically impossible survival rates' in camp conditions." Anton's voice carried a carefully controlled fury. "They're being transferred to a facility outside Munich for 'enhanced evaluation of unusual genetic factors.'"

Greta felt the world tilt around her as the implications became clear. The Nazis had discovered gifted children in their camps and were preparing to study them like laboratory animals. Every instinct inherited from generations of covenant training screamed at her to maintain secrecy, to protect the larger secret even at the cost of individual lives. But these were children—gifted children whose only crime was being born into families targeted for genocide.

"We have to help them," she said, the words emerging before conscious thought could stop them.

Anton studied her face with eyes that seemed to see straight through to her soul. "Help them how? Walk invisible into a heavily guarded Nazi research facility and extract supernatural children whose very existence violates everything we've been taught about the need for secrecy?"

"Yes," Greta said, surprised by the certainty in her own voice. "Exactly that."

"And when our intervention is discovered? When reports circulate about impossible escapes and guards who swear they were attacked by invisible assailants? When Himmler's obsession with the occult is validated by evidence that supernatural abilities actually exist?"

The questions hung in the air between them like accusations. Anton was voicing every argument Greta's grandmother had made about the dangers of revelation, every reason why the covenant had spent six hundred years teaching its members to remain hidden regardless of the cost to individual lives.

But looking at the transport schedules in Anton's hands, thinking about gifted children being shipped to Nazi laboratories for dissection and experimentation, Greta found those arguments losing their power to restrain her.

"What if the covenant is wrong?" she asked quietly. "What if the catastrophic future my grandmother warned about is less certain than the catastrophic present we're living through right now?"

Anton was quiet for a long moment, his gaze shifting between the documents and Greta's face. When he finally spoke, his voice carried the weight of someone making a decision that would echo through generations.

"My unit is planning an operation in Munich next week," he said. "Officially, it's reconnaissance for a potential sabotage mission. Unofficially..." He met her eyes with an expression that was part challenge, part invitation. "I think I could use the assistance of someone who can walk unseen through impossible places."

Greta felt something shift inside her chest, as if a weight she had carried all her life was finally beginning to lift. "My resistance cell moves Jews through Berlin every week. We have safe houses, escape routes, contacts in neutral territories."

"Then perhaps it's time we discovered what the covenant's training is actually worth when applied to protecting the innocent rather than preserving organizational secrets."

As they prepared to leave Konrad's study—Anton with his stolen intelligence, Greta with the beginning of a plan that would either save gifted children or doom them all—neither could have predicted that their partnership would become something more than a temporary alliance of convenience.

Outside, Berlin lay under the bomber's moon that illuminated a city slowly consuming itself in service to evil. In hidden rooms and forgotten corners, resistance cells planned small acts of defiance against overwhelming darkness. And in places like Wannsee, men in uniforms continued to organize horror with the bureaucratic efficiency that had made the impossible into the routine.

But for the first time since her grandmother's death, Greta Müller felt something that might have been hope. She was no longer alone in carrying the burden of inherited gifts and inherited restrictions. She had found someone who understood both the power they carried and the impossible choices that power demanded.

Whether that understanding would lead to salvation or catastrophe remained to be seen. But as she faded back into invisibility and prepared to slip through Berlin's darkened streets, Greta knew she was finally ready to discover which mattered more: the covenant's ancient fear of revelation or the immediate demands of conscience.

The choice, like everything else in her hidden life, would be made in shadows. But for once, those shadows felt less like a prison and more like the first step toward light.

CHAPTER 11: THE UNKILLABLE SOLDIER

Munich, Germany

December 1943

The bullet should have killed Anton Volkov.

He felt it coming three seconds before the SS sniper pulled the trigger—a familiar whisper of future pain that had kept him alive through Stalingrad, the siege of Leningrad, and a dozen other battles where ordinary men had died by the thousands. The precognitive flash showed him the trajectory: a shot aimed at his heart from the bell tower of St. Peter's church, fired by a man whose hands shook from too much schnapps and too little sleep.

Anton threw himself sideways just as the rifle cracked, but even his supernatural reflexes couldn't completely evade a shot he had seen too late. The bullet meant for his heart took him in the left shoulder instead, spinning him around and slamming him against the brick wall of the alley where he had been observing the heavily guarded facility that housed Himmler's "special collection."

Blood soaked through his stolen Wehrmacht uniform as Anton pressed himself into the shadows, fighting to remain conscious while his body began the impossible work of healing. The bullet had shattered his collarbone and nicked an artery, injuries that should have left him dying in a Munich alley. Instead, he felt the familiar burning sensation that accompanied his gift's activation—bone knitting back together, blood vessels reconnecting, torn muscle regenerating at a rate that defied every law of biology.

It had been like this since childhood, though it had taken a war to reveal the true extent of what he could survive.

Kursk, July 1943. Five months earlier.

The memory surfaced with crystal clarity as Anton's body repaired itself in the Munich alley. He had been leading a reconnaissance patrol deep behind German lines when the Stuka dive bombers found them. The screaming engines, the whistle of falling bombs, the earth erupting in fountains of flame and shrapnel—and through it all, the precognitive flashes that let him see death approaching three seconds before it arrived.

He had saved four of his men by shouting warnings at precisely the right moments, pulling them away from impacts they couldn't see coming. But the fifth bomb, the one that landed directly in their foxhole, had been too close and too powerful for even supernatural reflexes to evade.

Anton remembered the moment of impact: a wall of fire and pressure that turned the world into chaos, shrapnel tearing through his body like hot knives, the certainty that he was about to die thousands of miles from the Siberian village where he had been

137

born. Then darkness, and the strange sensation of floating above his own mangled corpse while ghostly figures argued in voices he couldn't quite understand.

When he regained consciousness three days later, buried under rubble and surrounded by the bodies of his patrol, Anton discovered that dying was apparently something his body simply refused to do. The shrapnel wounds had healed, leaving only pale scars. The internal bleeding had stopped. Even his uniform had somehow repaired itself, as if reality itself was reluctant to acknowledge that Anton Volkov could be killed.

That was when he understood what his grandfather's whispered stories had really meant.

Present: Munich alley.

The shoulder wound finished healing with a final pulse of supernatural fire, leaving Anton whole and functional but deeply troubled by what he had observed during his reconnaissance. The facility across the street was no ordinary research installation. Even from a distance, his enhanced senses could detect the presence of others like himself—gifted individuals whose supernatural signatures called out to him like voices in the darkness.

But these weren't free agents choosing their own paths. They were prisoners, and from what Anton could sense of their conditions, they were being subjected to experiments that would have horrified even the most callous Soviet commissar.

The facility's official designation was "Ahnenerbe Forschungsgruppe H"—Ancestral Heritage Research Group H—but the intelligence reports Anton had stolen from various sources painted a different picture. This was Heinrich Himmler's attempt to create supernatural soldiers for the Reich, using captured gifted individuals as both test subjects and raw material for a breeding program designed to weaponize inherited abilities.

Anton checked his watch and settled deeper into the shadows to observe the facility's evening shift change. Guards emerged from the main building with the casual efficiency of men accustomed to routine, but Anton noticed something that made his blood run cold: several of the departing personnel showed signs of supernatural enhancement themselves. Enhanced strength, evidenced by the way they moved heavy equipment without apparent effort. Unnatural sensory awareness, suggested by the way they consistently looked in the right direction before sounds occurred. One guard seemed to anticipate questions before they were asked, responding to his colleague's unspoken thoughts.

The Nazis weren't just studying the gifted—they were successfully creating them.

The implications were staggering. If Himmler's researchers had found ways to artificially induce supernatural abilities, or worse, to transfer them from captured subjects to willing recipients, then the

139

covenant's most fundamental fear was becoming reality. Not through revelation to the general population, but through military weaponization by a regime that had already demonstrated its willingness to pursue any atrocity in service to ideology.

Anton's precognitive gift whispered a warning just before the patrol found him. Three SS soldiers, moving through the alley with the methodical precision of men conducting a security sweep. Unlike the guards at the facility, these appeared to be ordinary humans, but they were well-trained and heavily armed.

The first soldier rounded the corner just as Anton faded back into the deeper shadows, but his movement had been spotted. A shout in German, the sound of weapons being readied, boots pounding on cobblestones as the patrol converged on his position.

Anton could have fought them. His gift didn't just make him difficult to kill—it also provided tactical advantages that no ordinary soldier could match. Three seconds of warning about every attack, every movement, every intention meant that he could dance through combat like a man fighting blind children. But killing German soldiers in the middle of Munich would only draw more attention to himself and potentially compromise his mission.

Instead, he chose a different approach.

The first soldier to enter the alley found it empty except for shadows and the faint smell of blood. Anton pressed himself against the wall just inside the entrance, invisible in the darkness, as the patrol searched the space he had vacated. His healing gift had worked well enough to stop the bleeding entirely, leaving no trail for them to follow.

"Nothing here," one of the soldiers reported to his sergeant. "Probably just cats fighting over scraps."

"Check the other side of the building," the sergeant ordered. "Command reported possible infiltrator activity in this sector."

As the patrol moved on, Anton remained motionless in his hiding place, thinking about what he had observed and what it meant for the mission he and Greta had planned. The facility was more heavily guarded than their intelligence had suggested, and some of those guards possessed abilities that would make a conventional rescue operation virtually impossible.

But there was something else—something that made his decision to help Greta rescue the captured children feel less like a violation of covenant principles and more like a desperate necessity. Through his supernatural senses, Anton had detected a familiar signature among the prisoners: the distinctive golden thread that marked someone from his own bloodline.

His sister Katarina, missing for two years since her Red Army unit had been overrun near Kharkov, was somewhere inside that facility.

The realization changed everything. What had begun as a partnership with a German resistance operative based on shared supernatural heritage had become deeply personal. Anton's commitment to the covenant's secrecy had been absolute until he discovered that his own family was being used as raw material for Nazi supernatural experiments.

As he prepared to leave his hiding place and return to the safe house where Greta was waiting for his report, Anton reflected on the impossible position in which all gifted individuals found themselves. The covenant demanded secrecy above all else, even at the cost of individual lives. But what happened when that secrecy became not just personally costly but actively counterproductive? When hiding from the world's attention only made it easier for those who discovered the truth to exploit and abuse the gifted without consequence?

His grandfather, like Greta's grandmother, had filled Anton's childhood with stories about Eleanor Blackthorne's vision and the catastrophic future that awaited if supernatural abilities became widely known. But as Anton made his way through Munich's darkened streets, avoiding patrols and checkpoints with preternatural ease, he found himself questioning whether that future was really worse than the present reality.

The Nazis had discovered the gifted anyway, despite centuries of careful concealment. They were conducting experiments that would make supernatural abilities into weapons of mass destruction, using innocent people as test subjects and breeding stock. The very thing the covenant existed to prevent was happening under cover of a war that provided perfect camouflage for atrocities.

How many more gifted individuals were being held in similar facilities across the Reich? How many others like Katarina had disappeared into the machinery of supernatural weaponization? And how long before the covenant's policy of non-interference became indistinguishable from complicity in genocide?

By the time Anton reached the resistance safe house—a bombed-out bakery in the Schwabing district where Greta had established their temporary headquarters—his mind was made up. The covenant's ancient obligations to secrecy were important, but they could not be allowed to supersede the immediate moral obligation to protect innocent lives.

Greta looked up from the maps and documents she had been studying as Anton entered through the bakery's concealed rear entrance. The invisible woman had materialized into visibility upon hearing his approach, but Anton could see the strain that maintaining her gift for extended periods was beginning to place on her. There were dark circles under her eyes, and her hands showed the slight tremor that came from supernatural abilities pushed beyond their natural limits.

"You're injured," she said immediately, noting the blood on his uniform despite the healed shoulder beneath.

"Was injured. I heal quickly, remember?" Anton moved to the table where Greta had spread building plans, guard schedules, and transport records stolen from various Nazi sources. "What I found changes our approach significantly."

"How so?"

"The facility isn't just holding gifted children for study. They're using them to create enhanced soldiers." Anton pointed to the main building on the architectural plans. "Some of the guards I observed tonight showed clear signs of supernatural abilities. The Nazis aren't just studying our gifts—they're successfully transferring them to their own personnel."

Greta's face went pale. "That should be impossible. Supernatural abilities are inherited, not acquired."

"Should be, yes. But Himmler's researchers have apparently found ways to make the impossible routine." Anton pulled out the photographs he had taken of the guard rotation. "Look at the movement patterns. Several of these men are demonstrating enhanced reflexes, unusual strength, possibly even precognitive abilities."

"And the children?"

"Still there. Still alive, as far as I can determine." Anton hesitated, then decided to share the personal stake that had solidified his commitment to their mission. "Including someone from my own family. My sister Katarina."

Greta's expression shifted from concern to understanding. "This isn't just about saving innocent children anymore."

"It never was just about that," Anton replied. "But yes, it's personal now. Which means I'm committed to this rescue regardless of the consequences for covenant secrecy."

"And if our intervention exposes the existence of supernatural abilities to the world? If it triggers the catastrophic revelation your family trained you to prevent?"

Anton looked around the destroyed bakery, its walls scorched by bombs and its windows boarded against the winter cold. Outside, a city slowly starved under the weight of a war that had already claimed millions of lives and showed no signs of ending. The catastrophic future the covenant feared was beginning to seem less terrible than the catastrophic present they were already living through.

"Then perhaps," he said quietly, "it's time we discovered whether our ancestors' vision of the future was prophecy or just fear disguised as wisdom."

As they bent over the building plans and began to sketch out a rescue operation that would either save innocent lives or doom humanity to supernatural warfare, Anton felt the weight of six centuries of inherited obligation settling on his shoulders. But for the first time in his life, that weight felt less like a burden and more like a challenge—a test of whether the covenant's principles could evolve to meet circumstances that Eleanor Blackthorne could never have imagined.

The choice between secrecy and action, between inherited wisdom and immediate necessity, would define not just their mission but the future of everyone who carried the burden of supernatural gifts in a world gone mad with ordinary evil.

Outside, Munich slept fitfully under the threat of Allied bombers, while in hidden facilities throughout the Reich, gifted individuals endured experiments that transformed them from people into weapons. The war between nations would eventually end, but the war for the soul of the supernatural community was just beginning.

CHAPTER 12: CROSSING PATHS

Berlin, Germany

January 1944

The assassination attempt was supposed to be impossible.

Greta crouched invisible on the roof of the Reich Chancellery, watching through the skylight as Adolf Hitler paced before a map of the Eastern Front, his hands gesturing frantically as he berated his generals about the retreat from Leningrad. Below her, separated by nothing more than a pane of glass and thirty feet of air, was the man whose death could end the war and save millions of lives.

All she had to do was become visible for ten seconds, drop through the skylight, and put a knife in the Führer's neck before his bodyguards could react. Her invisibility would make escape equally simple—chaos in the aftermath, perhaps a few wild shots from confused guards, but nothing that could threaten someone who could fade from sight at will.

The temptation was overwhelming. Every moral instinct, every fiber of resistance training, every memory of the atrocities she had witnessed screamed at her to act. Here was the source of so much evil, vulnerable and unaware, protected only by ordinary security measures that her supernatural gift could easily circumvent.

But forty feet away, crouched behind a ventilation unit on the same roof, Anton Volkov was experiencing the same terrible temptation—and the same crushing weight of inherited obligation that demanded he do nothing.

Their eyes met across the rooftop, two gifted individuals from opposite sides of the war, united in their supernatural heritage and their shared burden of knowing they could change history with a single act of violence. Anton's presence was supposed to be a complication—he was Soviet intelligence, she was German resistance, their nations were allies but their agendas were different. Instead, his arrival had crystallized the moral crisis that had been building in Greta's mind for months.

The original plan had been simple: Greta would use her invisibility to plant explosives in the Reich Chancellery's foundation, creating an "accident" that would kill Hitler while appearing to be the result of Allied bombing. Clean, deniable, with no supernatural implications that might attract unwanted attention. Anton's mission was parallel but separate—he was supposed to eliminate Heinrich Himmler during the same meeting, using his precognitive abilities to ensure a perfect shot from a sniper's position.

But as they watched their targets through the glass below, both realized they were facing the moment that every member of Eleanor's covenant dreaded: the choice between using their gifts to prevent immediate evil or maintaining the secrecy that preserved humanity from a greater catastrophe.

Anton moved first, abandoning his sniper's position to approach Greta's location with the silent efficiency of someone whose supernatural reflexes made ordinary stealth seem clumsy by comparison. His presence beside her was warm and solid in the January cold, a reminder that she was not the only one carrying an impossible burden.

"We could end it tonight," he whispered, his voice barely audible above the wind that swept across the Chancellery's roof. "Both of them. Hitler, Himmler, perhaps others. The war would collapse within months."

"And when the investigations begin?" Greta replied, though she didn't move from her position overlooking the skylight. "When witnesses describe impossible events, when security footage shows attacks by invisible assailants? When the surviving Nazis claim their leaders were killed by supernatural forces?"

"Would anyone believe them?"

It was a good question. The Nazi obsession with occult symbolism and mystical nonsense had made their leadership seem prone to superstitious explanations for ordinary events. Perhaps reports of supernatural assassination would be dismissed as the desperate fantasies of a collapsing regime.

But even as Greta considered the possibility, her grandmother's voice echoed in her memory: "The revelation of our gifts always begins with small exposures, singular incidents that seem dismissible in isolation. But patterns emerge, questions multiply, and eventually someone with resources and intelligence pieces together the truth. When that happens, the cascade cannot be stopped."

"My family has records," Anton said quietly, as if reading her thoughts. "Documents dating back to the original covenant. There are examples of what happens when individual members break secrecy for supposedly noble purposes."

"Such as?"

"A healer in Renaissance Italy who revealed himself to save a city from plague. Within a decade, the Papal Inquisition was conducting systematic hunts for others like him, torturing and executing anyone suspected of supernatural abilities. The resulting persecutions killed more gifted individuals than the plague ever could have."

Greta felt her resolve wavering as she listened to Anton's warning, but the sight of Hitler below—animated with passion as he planned new atrocities—made it difficult to focus on theoretical future consequences when immediate evil was so tangible and present.

"And if we do nothing?" she asked. "How many millions die while we preserve our precious secrecy?"

Anton was quiet for a long moment, his gaze shifting between Hitler and the darkness beyond the Chancellery's walls. When he spoke again, his voice carried a weight that seemed too heavy for one person to bear.

"There's something else," he said. "Something I discovered in the family archives that I haven't shared with anyone. About this war, about how it began."

"What do you mean?"

Anton reached into his coat and withdrew a leather portfolio, its contents protected by multiple layers of oiled cloth. "Documents from the 1920s and 1930s. Correspondence between covenant families across Europe. Planning sessions for something they called 'Operation Prometheus.'"

The name meant nothing to Greta, but the careful way Anton handled the documents suggested their contents were both precious and dangerous. He selected a single sheet of paper and handed it to her—a letter written in German, dated 1932, signed with initials she didn't recognize.

"Read the third paragraph," Anton instructed.

Greta squinted at the careful script in the dim light from the Chancellery below. The words made her blood run cold:

"The Austrian subject continues to demonstrate promising instability and resentment toward existing power structures. Our operatives in Munich report that his rhetoric regarding supernatural themes is becoming more extreme, which serves our purposes perfectly. When he inevitably rises to power, his occult obsessions will discredit any genuine supernatural revelations that might emerge during his regime. The chaos of the resulting conflict will also provide cover for necessary 'adjustments' to problematic bloodlines."

"They're talking about Hitler," Greta whispered, the implications hitting her like a physical blow.

"Among others. Stalin received similar 'guidance' from Soviet covenant members. Mussolini was influenced by operatives in Rome. The entire war..." Anton's voice trailed off, leaving the horrific conclusion unspoken.

"The covenant engineered World War II?"

"Not engineered, exactly. But influenced, guided, shaped to serve their purposes." Anton retrieved the letter and returned it to his portfolio. "The thinking was that a massive, chaotic conflict would accomplish several objectives simultaneously. Discredit occult beliefs through association with obvious madmen. Provide cover for the elimination of problematic gifted bloodlines. Create conditions where genuine supernatural events could be dismissed as wartime propaganda or hysteria."

152

Greta stared down at Hitler, who was now shouting at a general whose face had gone pale with fear. The man whose death she was contemplating was not just a spontaneous evil that had emerged from historical circumstances, but at least partially a creation of the very organization she had been raised to serve.

"How many people have died because of covenant manipulation?" she asked.

"Tens of millions, probably. The Holocaust alone..." Anton's expression was grim. "Our family records suggest that the Nazis' decision to target Jewish populations was influenced by covenant intelligence about bloodlines with high concentrations of supernatural genes. They turned the Reich's extermination apparatus into a tool for what they called 'genetic housekeeping.'"

The revelation was too enormous to process immediately. Everything Greta thought she understood about the war, about her role as a resistance fighter, about the moral clarity of opposing the Nazis, was suddenly complicated by the knowledge that her own organization had helped create the conflict she was fighting against.

"Then this is our fault," she said numbly. "All of it. The deaths, the genocide, the destruction—it's all the result of covenant attempts to prevent Eleanor's vision."

"Some of it, yes. But not all." Anton moved closer to the skylight, studying the scene below with the focused attention of someone preparing for action. "Which raises an interesting question: if the covenant's attempts to prevent catastrophe have caused a different catastrophe, what happens if we choose to act according to our own moral judgment rather than inherited obligation?"

Greta understood what he was suggesting. The covenant had spent six hundred years trying to prevent the supernatural revelation that Eleanor had seen in her vision. But their efforts had apparently created disasters that were arguably worse than anything in Eleanor's prophecy. Perhaps it was time to test whether direct action might produce better results than continued manipulation.

"You're proposing we kill Hitler?"

"I'm proposing we save the children in Himmler's facility first, and then decide whether the covenant's version of protecting humanity is actually worth preserving." Anton checked his watch. "The operation window closes in thirty minutes. After that, security changes shifts and our intelligence becomes useless."

Below them, Hitler had moved away from the map table and was approaching the windows that faced toward the bunker complex where Greta knew the "special prisoners" were being held. For a moment, the Führer's face was clearly visible through the skylight—pale, animated with fanatic energy, utterly human despite the inhuman ideology he represented.

Greta could have dropped through the glass at that moment. Ten seconds of visibility, one precise movement, and the war would have taken a very different course. But as she prepared to act, her supernatural senses detected something that made her freeze in position.

Hitler wasn't alone in the room below. Standing in the shadows near the door was a figure whose presence made Greta's gifted awareness recoil with recognition and revulsion. Tall, thin, dressed in the black uniform of the SS, but carrying an aura of supernatural power that was both familiar and terrifyingly wrong.

"Anton," she whispered urgently. "There's someone else down there. Someone like us."

Anton's expression darkened as he followed her gaze. "SS-Oberführer Wolfgang Kessler. One of Himmler's pet projects—a covenant member who was 'turned' during interrogation three years ago."

"Turned?"

"Convinced to serve the Reich in exchange for promises about the future management of supernatural bloodlines. He's the one providing intelligence about gifted families to the extermination squads." Anton's voice carried a hatred more personal than anything Greta had heard from him before. "He's also the reason my sister was captured."

The presence of a corrupted covenant member in Hitler's inner circle changed everything. This wasn't just about preventing immediate evil or maintaining ancient obligations—it was about confronting the reality that their own organization had been infiltrated and compromised at the highest levels.

"If we kill Hitler now, with Kessler watching, he'll know that other covenant members were responsible," Greta realized. "He'll report it to his handlers, both Nazi and supernatural. The exposure we're trying to prevent will happen anyway."

"Unless we kill him too," Anton suggested grimly.

"Two impossible assassinations in one night? That would guarantee investigation by every intelligence agency in Europe. And if either of us is captured..."

"Then we rescue the children first, as planned, and deal with the larger implications afterward." Anton began moving toward the roof access that would take them to the facility's underground levels. "Whatever the covenant has become, whatever compromises it has made, there are still innocent people depending on us to act."

As they prepared to abandon their assassination opportunity and focus on the rescue mission that had brought them together, Greta found herself thinking about Eleanor Blackthorne's original vision. Had the founder of their covenant foreseen that her efforts to prevent supernatural revelation would eventually create a conspiracy so vast and morally compromised that it became indistinguishable from the very evil it was meant to oppose?

The questions would have to wait. Below in the Chancellery's depths, gifted children were being prepared for experiments that would either kill them or transform them into weapons. Whatever the larger implications of covenant politics and historical manipulation, the immediate moral imperative was clear.

They would save the innocent first, and sort out the consequences of six centuries of misguided wisdom later.

But as Greta faded into invisibility and followed Anton toward their real target, she carried with her the growing certainty that the war they were fighting was not the one they had been trained for. The enemy was not just the Nazis, or even the corrupted covenant members who served them, but the entire system of inherited assumptions that had led the gifted to believe that secrecy was always preferable to action.

Tonight would test whether that belief was wisdom or merely the accumulated fear of generations who had forgotten that some things were worth fighting for, regardless of the consequences.

The choice between hiding and acting, between preserving secrets and protecting lives, would define not just their mission but the future of everyone who carried the burden of supernatural gifts in a world that had apparently never been as ignorant of their existence as they had believed.

CHAPTER 13: THE WEIGHT OF HISTORY

Berlin, Germany

February 1944

The classified documents spread across the table in their safe house painted a picture of the world that neither Greta nor Anton had been prepared to confront. Three weeks of careful intelligence gathering, of risks taken and sources cultivated, had yielded information that transformed their understanding of the war and their place within it.

Greta stared at the decoded telegraph intercepts between Washington and London, her hands trembling slightly as she read the words that shattered her remaining illusions about covenant secrecy:

CHURCHILL TO ROOSEVELT - 15 FEB 1944

REGARDING YOUR INQUIRY ABOUT 'SPECIAL ASSETS' - BRITISH INTELLIGENCE CONFIRMS EXISTENCE OF ENHANCED INDIVIDUALS ON ALL SIDES OF CONFLICT. SUGGEST COORDINATION OF COUNTER-SUPERNATURAL PROTOCOLS WITH YOUR MAN DONOVAN. THE RUSSIANS CLEARLY HAVE THEIR OWN PROGRAM. RECOMMEND EXTREME CAUTION IN DEPLOYMENT OF OUR ASSETS.

ROOSEVELT TO CHURCHILL - 16 FEB 1944

OSS REPORTS SUCCESSFUL IDENTIFICATION OF GERMAN SUPERNATURAL PROJECTS. HIMMLER'S FACILITIES CONTAIN MORE THAN EXPECTED. OUR PHILADELPHIA EXPERIMENT YIELDING PROMISING RESULTS. STALIN'S LAST COMMUNICATION MENTIONED 'SPECIAL SOLDIERS' AT STALINGRAD. THIS KNOWLEDGE CHANGES EVERYTHING.

Anton looked up from the Soviet documents he had been translating, his face pale with a mixture of anger and despair. "It's worse than we thought. Much worse."

Greta set down the Allied intercepts and moved to where Anton sat surrounded by papers that bore the seal of the NKVD. "What did you find?"

"My grandfather's real work for the Soviet Union." Anton's voice was hollow as he gestured toward the documents. "I always knew he was involved in intelligence, but I thought it was ordinary espionage. Instead..." He picked up a thick file marked with Cyrillic characters. "Project Bogatyr. A systematic program to identify, capture, and weaponize supernatural individuals that began in 1922."

"Weaponize how?"

"Read this." Anton handed her a translated report dated 1939. "Field test results from the Finnish border. Three soldiers with enhanced abilities—one healer, one with superhuman strength, one who could sense enemy positions through supernatural awareness. Deployed against a Finnish machine gun nest that had been holding up an entire Soviet division."

Greta read with growing horror as the clinical language described the systematic use of gifted individuals as living weapons. The healer had been sent to retrieve wounded soldiers from no-man's land, drawing enemy fire that revealed sniper positions. The strong man had lifted and hurled artillery shells like grenades. The sensor had guided night raids with supernatural precision.

"All three were killed within a week," Anton continued. "Not by enemy action, but by NKVD execution squads. The report concludes that enhanced soldiers are too dangerous to allow survival after their usefulness ends."

"And your grandfather participated in this?"

"Organized it." Anton's hands clenched into fists as he spoke. "Alexei Volkov, Hero of the Soviet Union, devoted communist, systematic betrayer of his own kind. He used his knowledge of covenant bloodlines to identify targets for recruitment. When they refused to serve, they were eliminated. When they complied, they were used until they broke, then eliminated anyway."

161

Greta felt the familiar weight of inherited betrayal settling on her shoulders. First the revelation that the covenant had helped engineer the war, now the discovery that supernatural programs existed on all sides of the conflict, run by people who apparently knew exactly what they were dealing with.

"The secrecy was never real, was it?" she said quietly. "The governments have known about us all along."

"Some of them, yes. The intelligence agencies, certain military units, selected political leaders." Anton gathered the Soviet documents into a neat pile, as if organizing them could somehow organize the chaos in his mind. "But knowledge isn't the same as revelation. A few dozen people in each government knowing about supernatural abilities is different from public awareness."

"Is it?" Greta moved to the window, looking out at Berlin's war-torn streets where ordinary citizens went about their daily struggle for survival, unaware of the invisible conflict being waged above their heads. "If Roosevelt and Churchill and Stalin all know about the gifted, if they're already running programs to weaponize supernatural abilities, then what exactly are we preserving by maintaining secrecy?"

It was the question that had been gnawing at both of them since they discovered the scope of governmental knowledge about their abilities. The covenant's fundamental justification—that revelation would lead to catastrophic warfare between the gifted and ungifted—seemed increasingly hollow when the warfare was already happening, hidden behind layers of classification and plausible deniability.

"There's something else," Anton said, his voice heavy with reluctance. "Something I found in my family's personal archives that explains why the covenant continues to insist on secrecy even when governments already know the truth."

He withdrew a leather journal from his coat, its pages yellowed with age and marked with the careful script of someone writing in multiple languages. "My great-grandfather's account of the 1918 influenza pandemic."

"What does that have to do with supernatural secrecy?"

"Everything." Anton opened the journal to a page marked with a red ribbon. "The influenza wasn't entirely natural. It was the result of a failed covenant experiment in biological manipulation, an attempt to create a 'manageable catastrophe' that would distract world attention from emerging supernatural activity."

Greta felt her blood turn to ice. "The covenant created the Spanish Flu?"

"Not intentionally. They were trying to develop a limited plague that would justify the establishment of international health monitoring systems—systems that could identify and track gifted bloodlines under the cover of public health initiatives." Anton's finger traced the careful script as he read. "But the biological agent mutated beyond their control. Fifty million people died because covenant scientists thought they could engineer a controllable disaster."

The numbers were too vast to process emotionally. Fifty million people—more than all the casualties of the current war combined—dead because the gifted had tried to manipulate history to serve their vision of necessary secrecy.

"And this is why we're supposed to maintain the covenant's policies?" Greta asked, though she already knew the answer.

"This is why they believe any direct intervention is too dangerous to risk." Anton closed the journal with the careful reverence of someone handling a holy relic. "Every time the gifted have tried to actively shape world events, the unintended consequences have been catastrophic. The 1918 pandemic. The economic collapse of 1929, which was triggered by covenant members trying to manipulate financial markets to prevent the rise of extremist political movements. And now this war, which began as an attempt to create controlled chaos and became something far worse."

Greta turned away from the window and sank into a chair, feeling the weight of six centuries of accumulated failure and good intentions gone horribly wrong. Every major disaster of the past hundred years, it seemed, could be traced back to covenant attempts to prevent Eleanor's vision from coming to pass.

"So what do we do?" she asked. "Continue to serve an organization that has apparently caused more suffering than it has prevented? Or risk making things even worse by acting on our own judgment?"

Before Anton could answer, a knock at the safe house door made both of them freeze in alarm. Three quick raps, followed by two, then one—the signal they had arranged with Klaus's resistance cell for emergency contact. But Klaus wasn't due to check on them for another two days.

Anton moved to the door with supernatural caution, his enhanced senses probing the area beyond for signs of threat or deception. What he found was something worse than Nazi patrols or Gestapo raids: the familiar golden signature of another covenant member, someone whose power felt both alien and achingly familiar.

"Open the door, brother," came a voice from the hallway, speaking in the Russian dialect of Anton's childhood. "We need to talk."

Anton exchanged a glance with Greta, who had faded partially invisible as a precautionary measure. Then, against every instinct for self-preservation, he opened the door to reveal a woman who looked so much like him that there could be no question of her identity.

Katarina Volkova stood in the hallway, wearing the uniform of an SS auxiliary but carrying herself with the careful poise of someone who had survived experiences that should have broken her. Her face bore the pale scars of recent wounds, and her eyes held the particular depth that came from extended use of supernatural abilities under extreme stress.

"Hello, Anton," she said quietly. "I've been looking for you."

"Katya." Anton's voice broke slightly as he spoke his sister's childhood nickname. "We thought you were dead. The reports from Kharkov—"

"I was captured, not killed. Though I understand the confusion." Katarina entered the safe house uninvited, her gaze taking in the scattered intelligence documents with professional interest. "The past two years have been... educational."

Greta materialized fully, studying the newcomer with a mixture of relief and suspicion. This was the woman they had planned to rescue from Himmler's facility, but her presence here, in an SS uniform, wearing the confident bearing of someone who belonged in Nazi hierarchy, suggested that their intelligence had been incomplete.

"You escaped?" Greta asked.

"I was released," Katarina corrected. "After providing certain services to the Reich's supernatural research programs. Services that included identifying the location of resistance cells and the activities of Soviet agents operating in German territory."

The words hit Anton like a physical blow. "You betrayed us."

"I preserved us," Katarina replied calmly. "Do you have any idea what Himmler's scientists can do to gifted individuals who refuse to cooperate? The procedures they've developed for extracting supernatural abilities from unwilling subjects? The breeding programs designed to create weaponized children?"

She moved to the table where their intelligence documents were spread, picking up one of the Soviet files with familiar ease. "I chose cooperation over resistance because cooperation allowed me to survive with my abilities intact. And survival, brother, is what the covenant has always been about."

"Survival through collaboration with genocidal madmen?"

"Survival through pragmatic acceptance of reality." Katarina set down the Soviet document and faced both Anton and Greta with an expression that mixed love and pity in equal measure. "You think you're heroes, planning to rescue innocent children and expose Nazi supernatural programs. But you're actually about to trigger the very catastrophe that Eleanor's vision warned us about."

"How so?" Greta demanded.

"Because the balance is more delicate than you understand." Katarina gestured toward the Allied intercepts on the table.

"Roosevelt and Churchill know about supernatural abilities, yes, but their knowledge is limited and carefully controlled. A few intelligence officers, a handful of researchers, perhaps a dozen political leaders worldwide. The general population remains ignorant."

"And if we rescue the children?"

"Then you create evidence that cannot be ignored or suppressed. Dozens of witnesses to impossible escapes. Physical proof that supernatural abilities exist. Investigation by agencies that will demand answers." Katarina's voice carried the weight of someone who had seen the consequences of exposure firsthand. "Within months, every government on Earth will be demanding access to gifted individuals for their own programs. The arms race you think you're preventing will become inevitable."

Anton stared at his sister, seeing in her scarred face and confident bearing the shape of choices he might have made under different circumstances. "So we do nothing? We let innocent children be tortured and killed to preserve a secret that's already partially compromised?"

"We let history unfold as it must," Katarina replied. "The children in Himmler's facility will die, yes. But their deaths will be individual tragedies rather than the catalyst for a supernatural arms race that could destroy civilization."

The calculus was brutal in its simplicity. A few dozen lives weighed against the potential destruction of millions. Individual suffering measured against species survival. The same impossible choice that had defined the covenant for six centuries, presented in its starkest possible terms.

Greta looked around the safe house at the evidence of governmental knowledge, at the documents describing failed covenant interventions, at the sister whose survival had come at the cost of collaboration with evil. Everything pointed toward the same conclusion: that action, no matter how well-intentioned, carried risks that outweighed any possible benefit.

"Eleanor's vision," she said quietly. "What if it wasn't wrong? What if every time we try to prevent it, we just make it more likely to occur?"

"That's the question the covenant leadership has been wrestling with for generations," Katarina confirmed. "Every intervention creates new problems. Every attempt to shape history produces unintended consequences. Eventually, you have to ask whether the cure has become worse than the disease."

As evening fell over Berlin, casting the safe house into shadows that seemed to echo the moral darkness of their situation, Anton and Greta faced the final test of their commitment to inherited wisdom versus immediate conscience. Outside, children who shared their supernatural heritage were being prepared for experiments that would either kill them or transform them into weapons. The power to save those children lay within their grasp, requiring nothing more than the will to use their gifts openly.

But the weight of history—of 1918 pandemic deaths, of economic collapses, of wars that began as attempts to prevent greater wars—pressed down on them like the accumulated judgment of six centuries of failure and good intentions gone wrong.

"We walk away," Anton said finally, his voice hollow with defeat. "We let the children die, we let the war continue its course, we preserve the secret that may already be meaningless."

"We trust Eleanor's vision over our own moral judgment," Greta agreed, though the words tasted like poison in her mouth. "We choose the survival of the species over the survival of individuals."

It was the choice their ancestors had made, generation after generation, always with the promise that their sacrifice was necessary, that their inaction preserved something more valuable than the lives they failed to save. But as they prepared to abandon Berlin and let history unfold without their intervention, both carried with them the growing certainty that the covenant's cure had indeed become worse than any disease Eleanor could have imagined.

The weight of history, it seemed, was too heavy for any individual conscience to bear. But history itself would judge whether their choice was wisdom or cowardice, and that judgment would echo through generations yet to come.

CHAPTER 14: CONSEQUENCES OF INACTION

Munich, Germany

May 8, 1945

The silence that followed Germany's surrender was deafening.

Greta Müller stood in the rubble of what had once been Himmler's research facility, watching Allied investigators catalog the horrors that had been hidden behind institutional walls and classification stamps. The building's underground levels had been thoroughly destroyed by retreating SS forces, but enough evidence remained to paint a picture of systematic atrocity that made even hardened war correspondents weep openly.

Thirty-seven children, the investigators reported. Ages ranging from six to sixteen, all showing signs of prolonged medical experimentation. All dead.

Greta closed her eyes and tried not to think about the fact that she could have saved them. That a single night's work eighteen months earlier could have emptied those cells and delivered those children to safety. That her invisible hands could have unlocked doors, disabled guards, guided innocents to freedom while their captors stared at empty air in confusion.

Instead, she had chosen the greater good. The preservation of humanity's ignorance. The maintenance of supernatural secrecy at the cost of individual lives.

The choice still felt like poison in her veins.

"The Americans are asking questions about the research program," Anton said quietly, approaching through the rubble with the careful step of someone who had learned to move silently through dangerous places. His Soviet uniform looked out of place among the Allied investigators, but his credentials as part of the joint intelligence mission gave him access to areas that were otherwise restricted.

"What kind of questions?"

"The useful kind." Anton handed her a classified document stamped with OSS markings. "They've found evidence of enhancement programs, references to 'acquired abilities,' documentation of experiments that shouldn't be scientifically possible. The intelligence community is starting to piece together the scope of what the Nazis were attempting."

Greta read through the report with growing unease. The Americans had indeed identified clear evidence of supernatural research, but their conclusions were both more and less dangerous than she had expected. More dangerous because they were taking the evidence seriously, treating it as a legitimate avenue for investigation rather than dismissing it as Nazi pseudoscience. Less dangerous because they were interpreting it through the lens of advanced technology rather than inherent human abilities.

"They think it was some kind of experimental drug therapy," she realized. "Chemical enhancement rather than genetic inheritance."

"For now, yes. But how long before someone asks the right questions? How long before they start looking for surviving test subjects who might demonstrate these abilities naturally?" Anton's expression was grim. "We bought time, Greta, but we didn't eliminate the threat of revelation."

The irony was bitter. They had sacrificed innocent lives to preserve a secret that was gradually unraveling anyway. Every month since the war's end had brought new questions, new investigations, new pieces of evidence that pointed toward the existence of supernatural abilities. The covenant's policy of absolute secrecy was failing incrementally, one classified report at a time.

But perhaps most crushing of all was the knowledge that their choice to remain hidden had accomplished nothing positive to balance against the lives they had failed to save.

"I've been reading the strategic assessments," Greta said quietly. "American and British intelligence estimates about how the war might have ended differently."

"And?"

"If Hitler had died in January 1944, when we had the chance to kill him, the war would have ended six months earlier. The Holocaust would have been interrupted before the final phase. Millions of people would have survived." She looked around at the destroyed facility, thinking of the children whose bodies had been removed just hours before. "Our decision to preserve supernatural secrecy may have prolonged human suffering rather than preventing it."

Anton nodded slowly, his face reflecting the same weight of realization that had been pressing down on Greta for months. "The covenant teaches that intervention always makes things worse. But they never consider that non-intervention can be just as destructive."

They stood together in the rubble, two people who had chosen inherited wisdom over immediate conscience and discovered that both paths led to moral catastrophe. Around them, Allied investigators continued their methodical documentation of Nazi atrocities, unaware that the evidence they were cataloging included crimes that could have been prevented by the very people who now watched their work.

"What will you do now?" Greta asked.

"Return to the Soviet Union. Continue my intelligence work under the assumption that supernatural abilities remain classified knowledge rather than public awareness." Anton's smile was bitter.

"Pretend that the choice we made was the right one, while carrying the knowledge that it probably wasn't."

"And if you're assigned to hunt other gifted individuals?"

"Then I'll remember that the covenant's definition of protection sometimes requires destruction, and I'll try to find ways to serve both masters without destroying what's left of my soul."

Greta understood the impossible position that awaited all covenant members in the post-war world. The governments knew about supernatural abilities now, but that knowledge was contained within intelligence agencies and classified research programs. The gifted would be valued as assets rather than feared as threats, but that value would make them prisoners in all but name.

They would serve their nations' interests while maintaining the fiction that they were simply enhanced humans rather than inherently supernatural beings. They would use their gifts in service to the very governments that would imprison or execute them if the full truth were revealed. And they would raise their children to carry the same impossible burdens, the same inherited obligations to secrecy and service.

"I'm pregnant," Greta said suddenly, the words emerging before she had consciously decided to share them.

Anton's expression shifted to something approaching wonder. "Congratulations. And condolences."

"Klaus's child. My brother didn't survive the liberation of Berlin, but..." She placed a hand over her still-flat abdomen, thinking about the life growing inside her and the world it would inherit. "The child will carry the bloodline. The gifts. The knowledge of what we are and what we've chosen not to do."

"What will you tell them? About the covenant, about the choices we've made?"

Greta was quiet for a long moment, watching American soldiers load classified documents into trucks bound for intelligence facilities where the evidence of supernatural research would disappear into filing cabinets and security vaults. Somewhere in those documents were the names of the children who had died in this facility, reduced to data points in reports that would never see public scrutiny.

"I'll tell them the truth," she said finally. "That we're part of an organization that began with noble intentions and has spent six centuries learning that noble intentions can lead to ignoble choices. That every generation inherits the mistakes of the previous one, and every generation has to decide whether to perpetuate those mistakes or risk making new ones."

"And if they choose differently than we did?"

"Then perhaps they'll be wiser than their parents. Or perhaps they'll simply discover new ways to be wrong." Greta turned away from the facility and began walking toward the Allied checkpoint where her resistance credentials would allow her to return to Berlin. "Either way, they'll have to live with the consequences of their choices, just as we have to live with ours."

As they prepared to part ways—perhaps forever—Anton reached into his coat and withdrew a leather journal similar to the one that had contained his family's dark history. "If your child inherits the gifts, if they need to understand the full scope of what they're inheriting, give them this."

Greta accepted the journal with hands that trembled slightly. "What is it?"

"Everything I learned about the covenant's true history. The 1918 pandemic, the manipulation of world events, the systematic betrayal of our own people. The next generation deserves to know what they're really signing up for when they inherit our obligations."

"And if that knowledge leads them to abandon the covenant entirely?"

"Then perhaps the covenant deserves to be abandoned." Anton's expression was infinitely sad. "Perhaps the greatest gift we can give our children is the freedom to choose differently than we did."

They embraced briefly, two people who had shared the weight of impossible choices and discovered that even the right choice could feel like betrayal. Then Anton walked toward the Soviet checkpoint while Greta made her way toward the American lines, carrying with her the beginning of a new life and the accumulated guilt of an old one.

Berlin, 1962

Seventeen years later, Greta sat in her small apartment in East Berlin, watching her teenage son Dmitri practice the careful control that would define the rest of his life. Unlike his mother's invisibility, Dmitri's gift manifested as an ability to sense and manipulate atomic structures—a power that had become both more relevant and more dangerous in the age of nuclear weapons.

"Tell me again about the choices," Dmitri said, his voice carrying the careful neutrality of someone who had learned that family history was a minefield of moral complexity. "About why you and my father's friend chose not to act."

Greta looked around their modest apartment, thinking about the life she had built in the shadow of her wartime choices. She had married a good man, a fellow resistance member who didn't know about her supernatural heritage. She had raised Dmitri with love and careful instruction about the burden he carried. And every day, she wondered whether the world would have been better or worse if she had chosen courage over caution in 1944.

"We chose to trust the wisdom of generations over the judgment of individuals," she said finally. "We believed that the covenant's experience with the consequences of revelation outweighed our immediate desire to save innocent lives."

"And now?"

"Now I wonder whether experience and wisdom are the same thing. Whether the patterns of the past necessarily predict the challenges of the future." Greta handed Dmitri the journal that Anton had given her at the war's end. "Your father's friend wanted you to have this when you were old enough to understand what it contains."

Dmitri accepted the journal with the reverence due to something that might reshape his understanding of the world. "What will I find in it?"

"Evidence that the covenant has been wrong before. Proof that our attempts to prevent catastrophe have sometimes caused greater catastrophes. Knowledge that might help you make better choices than your parents did."

As Dmitri opened the journal and began to read, Greta felt the weight of inherited guilt passing to the next generation. But for the first time since the war's end, she also felt something that might have been hope. Her son would face his own impossible choices, carry his own burden of supernatural responsibility, make his own decisions about when to act and when to remain hidden.

Perhaps he would be wiser than she had been. Perhaps he would find ways to serve both conscience and covenant. Or perhaps he would discover, as each generation seemed destined to do, that some burdens were too heavy for any individual to bear.

Outside, Berlin remained divided by walls both physical and ideological, a city that stood as testament to the consequences of human choices. And in apartments and houses around the world, other children of the gifted were inheriting the same impossible legacy, preparing to face a future where the ancient conflict between secrecy and service would take new forms but never truly end.

The weight of history pressed down on them all, but history, Greta had learned, was written by those brave enough—or foolish enough—to act despite that weight. Whether action or inaction served humanity better remained to be seen.

But the choice, as always, would belong to the next generation.

CHAPTER 15: THE NUCLEAR HEART

Chernobyl Nuclear Power Plant, Ukrainian SSR

April 25, 1986

Dmitri Petrov could feel the reactor's heartbeat through the concrete and steel that separated him from its radioactive core. The sensation was unlike anything an ordinary person could experience—a deep, thrumming pulse of atomic energy that resonated in his bones and whispered secrets about the fundamental forces that held matter together. To his supernatural senses, the Chernobyl Nuclear Power Plant was not just an industrial facility but a living entity whose vital signs told a story of growing instability.

And that story was becoming increasingly urgent.

Standing in the control room of Reactor 4, surrounded by the banks of gauges and switches that his colleagues trusted to monitor the reactor's condition, Dmitri felt the familiar weight of knowledge that he could never share. The instruments showed normal operation, parameters within acceptable ranges, no cause for concern. But his gift told a different story—one of microscopic fractures in fuel assemblies, of cooling systems operating at the edge of their design limits, of control rods that were developing hairline cracks that would soon compromise their ability to moderate the nuclear reaction.

"The test procedures are finalized for tonight's shutdown," announced Viktor Bryukhanov, the plant director, as he entered the control room with the confident bearing of a man whose faith in Soviet engineering was absolute. "We will demonstrate that our emergency cooling systems can operate independently of external power, as required by safety regulations."

Dmitri nodded along with the other engineers, though his supernatural awareness was screaming warnings about the proposed test. His gift allowed him to perceive the reactor's condition in ways that transcended instrumentation, and what he sensed filled him with dread. The reactor was already operating under stress, its internal structures weakened by months of pushing beyond safe parameters to meet production quotas. The planned test would place additional strain on systems that were barely holding together.

"Are we certain the reactor is in optimal condition for this test?" asked Anya Volkova, the reactor physicist whose sharp mind and careful attention to detail had made her invaluable to the plant's operations. Her question carried the careful neutrality of someone who had learned to phrase concerns in ways that wouldn't be interpreted as criticism of party directives.

Dmitri's heart clenched as he watched Anya study the instrument readings with the focused intensity that made her so effective at her job. Over the past six months, their professional relationship had evolved into something deeper—conversations that stretched beyond shift changes, shared meals in the plant cafeteria that became opportunities to discuss not just reactor physics but literature, music, dreams for the future. She was brilliant, dedicated, and utterly unaware that the man she was falling in love with carried the power to reach into the reactor's core with his mind and reshape the atomic forces that sustained the nuclear reaction.

"The reactor is operating within normal parameters," Bryukhanov replied, though Dmitri noticed the slight hesitation in his voice. Even without supernatural senses, experienced engineers could detect subtle signs that all was not well. "We have followed all prescribed procedures and safety protocols."

But procedures and protocols meant nothing when the underlying assumptions about reactor behavior were flawed. Dmitri could sense the specific ways in which the RBMK reactor design was vulnerable to catastrophic failure—positive void coefficients that would cause the reaction to accelerate rather than slow if cooling was lost, control rod designs that would briefly increase reactivity when inserted during emergency shutdown. These were engineering flaws that Soviet scientists had either ignored or concealed, flaws that transformed routine operations into games of nuclear roulette.

As the day shift concluded and the evening crew prepared for the test, Dmitri found himself walking with Anya through the corridors of the administrative building, their conversation touching on everything except the growing unease that both felt about the night's procedures.

"My grandmother used to tell stories about her work during the war," Anya said as they passed windows that offered views of the reactor buildings and cooling towers. "She was a mathematician, calculating artillery trajectories and supply logistics. She said the hardest part wasn't the complexity of the work, but the knowledge that small errors in her calculations could cost hundreds of lives."

Dmitri felt a chill of recognition. Anya was describing the same burden that had defined his entire life—the weight of knowledge and responsibility that came with the power to influence events on a massive scale. But where his gift was literal, hers was metaphorical; where his was hidden, hers was celebrated by the state.

"How did she handle that responsibility?" he asked.

"She said you do the best work you can with the information available, and you pray that you're not missing something crucial." Anya stopped walking and turned to face him, her expression serious. "Sometimes I think about that when I'm reviewing reactor data. What if there's something important that the instruments can't detect? What if we're missing warning signs that could prevent a catastrophe?"

The irony was overwhelming. Anya was describing exactly the situation they faced, asking precisely the right questions, but directed toward someone who possessed the very knowledge she feared they were missing. Dmitri could tell her everything—about the micro-fractures in the fuel assemblies, about the control rod degradation, about the cascade of failures that would unfold if the test proceeded as planned. But doing so would require explaining how he knew these things, and that explanation would shatter not just his own carefully constructed life but potentially the stability of the entire world.

"What would you do," Dmitri asked carefully, "if you discovered that you had access to information that could prevent a disaster, but sharing that information would destroy everything you cared about?"

Anya considered the question with the same methodical approach she brought to reactor physics. "I suppose it would depend on the scope of the disaster and the nature of what would be destroyed. Personal sacrifice to prevent greater suffering seems... necessary, even if it's also tragic."

Her answer was a knife in Dmitri's heart, both because it represented the moral clarity he craved and because it illustrated how impossible his situation truly was. Anya could speak of personal sacrifice in the abstract because she had no concept of what such sacrifice might entail for someone like him. She couldn't imagine the consequences that would follow if the world learned that people with supernatural abilities had been walking among them for centuries, influencing events, shaping history, concealing their true nature behind layers of secrecy and deception.

That evening, as the night shift prepared to conduct the fateful test, Dmitri took his position in the control room with the growing certainty that he was about to witness—and fail to prevent—a catastrophe that would echo through generations. His supernatural senses painted a detailed picture of the reactor's condition: fuel assemblies operating at temperature and pressure levels that exceeded safe parameters, coolant flow patterns that were creating hot spots in the core, control systems that were being pushed beyond their design limits.

The test began at 01:23 AM on April 26, 1986, with a series of procedures designed to simulate the loss of external electrical power. As Dmitri watched his colleagues manipulate controls and monitor instruments, he felt the reactor's response through his gift—a cascade of changes that the gauges couldn't detect but that his supernatural awareness perceived with terrifying clarity.

The emergency cooling pumps, running on generator power, were struggling to maintain adequate flow through the reactor core. The water level in the steam separators was dropping faster than anticipated. Most critically, the reactor's power output was becoming unstable, fluctuating in ways that indicated a loss of control that could quickly spiral into disaster.

"Power level is dropping below minimum operating parameters," reported Leonid Toptunov, the senior reactor control engineer, his voice carrying the first notes of concern.

Dmitri watched the readouts while simultaneously monitoring the reactor's true condition through his gift. The official instruments showed problematic but not immediately dangerous conditions. His supernatural senses revealed that they were minutes away from a cascade failure that would make Chernobyl synonymous with nuclear catastrophe.

He could stop it. The knowledge burned in his mind like radioactive fire. A subtle manipulation of the control rods, a slight adjustment to the cooling flow, a careful rebalancing of the nuclear reaction—any of these interventions would prevent the disaster while appearing to be the result of normal engineering procedures. His colleagues would believe they had successfully completed the test through skill and careful planning, never suspecting that supernatural intervention had saved them from catastrophe.

But such intervention would require the precise use of abilities that no human being should possess. And in a facility filled with scientists, engineers, and technicians trained to observe and analyze every aspect of reactor operation, the use of those abilities would eventually be detected and investigated.

"We should abort the test," Anya said quietly, her voice barely audible above the hum of machinery and the constant chatter of technical communication. She was studying instrument readings that looked normal to everyone else but that somehow triggered her intuitive understanding of complex systems. "Something doesn't feel right."

"The test parameters are within acceptable ranges," replied Alexander Akimov, the shift supervisor, though his tone suggested he shared Anya's unease. "We have authorization to proceed from plant management and the Ministry."

Dmitri closed his eyes and reached out with his supernatural senses, feeling the atomic-level processes that sustained the nuclear reaction. The reactor was balanced on a knife's edge, its stability maintained by feedback loops that were becoming increasingly fragile. In perhaps ten minutes, those feedback loops would fail catastrophically, and the resulting explosion would spread radioactive contamination across hundreds of miles of inhabited territory.

He could prevent it. The power was literally at his fingertips, requiring nothing more than the will to use it despite the consequences. But doing so would expose not just himself but potentially every member of the supernatural community that had remained hidden for over six centuries. The revelation of his abilities would trigger exactly the cascade of investigation and weaponization that Eleanor's covenant had been created to prevent.

"Dmitri." Anya's voice broke through his internal struggle. "You're pale. Are you feeling alright?"

He opened his eyes to find her studying him with the concerned attention of someone who had learned to read his moods and expressions. In her face, he saw not just professional worry but something deeper—the care of someone who had begun to envision a future that included him. They had talked recently about the possibility of transferring to other facilities, perhaps pursuing advanced degrees together, building a life that extended beyond the concrete walls and radioactive cores of nuclear engineering.

All of that would end if he used his gift to prevent the disaster. Anya would never understand why he had concealed his true nature, never forgive the deception that had formed the foundation of their relationship. The Soviet government would classify him as a strategic asset requiring permanent containment. The international community would demand access to supernatural abilities that could revolutionize everything from energy production to military applications.

The greater good demanded that he allow the disaster to unfold. The survival of the secret that protected humanity from supernatural warfare required the sacrifice of everyone who would suffer from radioactive contamination. The covenant's ancient wisdom, inherited across generations and written in the blood of those who had died to preserve it, commanded him to choose species survival over individual compassion.

But as Dmitri looked at Anya's face, thinking of the thousands of people sleeping peacefully in the nearby city of Pripyat, imagining the children who would develop cancer from exposure to radiation they could have been spared, the weight of inherited obligation felt less like wisdom and more like cowardice.

At 01:23:04, senior reactor control engineer Leonid Toptunov pressed the AZ-5 emergency shutdown button, initiating a procedure that should have safely terminated the nuclear reaction. Instead, the control rods' flawed design caused a brief spike in reactivity that overwhelmed the reactor's failing cooling systems.

Dmitri felt the moment of catastrophic failure like a physical blow— the sudden surge of nuclear energy, the rupture of cooling channels, the beginning of a steam explosion that would lift the reactor's 2,000-ton concrete lid and expose the burning graphite core to the atmosphere.

In that instant, with disaster literally seconds away, Dmitri Petrov made the choice that would define the rest of his life. He reached out with his supernatural gift and gently, carefully, precisely adjusted the flow of neutrons through the reactor core, dampening the runaway reaction and preventing the steam explosion that would have scattered radioactive debris across half of Europe.

To his colleagues, it appeared that the emergency shutdown had worked exactly as designed. The reactor powered down safely, the cooling systems maintained adequate flow, and the test concluded without incident. Only Dmitri knew that the successful shutdown had required intervention that no human being should have been capable of providing.

As the control room erupted in congratulations and relief, Anya caught his eye and smiled with the warm satisfaction of someone who had witnessed skilled professionals successfully navigate a challenging procedure. She had no idea that the man she was falling in love with had just used supernatural abilities to prevent one of the worst nuclear disasters in human history.

But Dmitri knew. And as he accepted the congratulations of his colleagues and participated in the routine post-test procedures, he carried with him the certain knowledge that his choice to act would eventually be discovered, investigated, and traced back to its impossible source.

He had saved thousands of lives and doomed himself in the process. The only question now was how long he could maintain the deception before the consequences of his choice caught up with him.

Outside, dawn was breaking over the city of Pripyat, where families were waking up to a morning they might never have lived to see without supernatural intervention. And in the control room of Reactor 4, Dmitri Petrov began the countdown to the end of the secret that had defined his family for generations.

The nuclear heart of Chernobyl continued to beat, steady and safe, its rhythm maintained by forces that science could not explain and the world was not yet ready to understand.

CHAPTER 16: FATHER'S SHADOW

Pripyat, Ukrainian SSR

May 15, 1986

The letter arrived three weeks after the test that never happened, delivered through official channels with the bureaucratic efficiency that marked all Soviet correspondence. Dmitri found it waiting on his desk when he returned from another routine shift at the reactor—routine because his supernatural intervention had ensured that the April test concluded without incident, leaving Chernobyl operating normally while the world remained ignorant of how close it had come to catastrophe.

The envelope bore the seal of the State Security Committee and was addressed to "Dmitri Antonovich Petrov"—a patronymic that made his blood run cold. Throughout his life, his mother had told him his father was a resistance fighter named Klaus who had died during the liberation of Berlin. She had never mentioned anyone named Anton, never explained why official documents sometimes bore a different patronymic than the one she used in daily conversation.

With trembling hands, Dmitri opened the envelope to find a single sheet of official letterhead and a small brass key:

Comrade Petrov,

Following the recent death of Senior Lieutenant Anton Mikhailovich Volkov, Hero of the Soviet Union, his personal effects have been transferred to state custody as required by security protocols. However, Lieutenant Volkov left specific instructions that certain items should be delivered to his son in the event of his death.

The enclosed key provides access to safety deposit box 247 at the State Bank, Pripyat branch. You are authorized to retrieve the contents within thirty days of this notification.

Glory to the Soviet Union.

The signature was illegible, buried beneath an official stamp that meant the letter had passed through multiple levels of bureaucratic approval. But what mattered wasn't the authorization—it was the revelation that his father had been alive until three weeks ago, and that he had been watching Dmitri closely enough to know exactly when his son might need access to family secrets.

That evening, after Anya had returned to her own apartment and the streets of Pripyat had settled into their usual quiet rhythm, Dmitri made his way to the State Bank. The building stood in the city center like a monument to Soviet financial planning, its concrete facade decorated with socialist realist sculptures that depicted workers building a glorious future through collective effort and individual sacrifice.

The bank clerk who assisted him was young and efficient, asking no questions about why someone would maintain a safety deposit box for decades only to have it claimed by a son who had never known his father existed. Such mysteries were common in the Soviet system, where family histories were often complicated by war, politics, and the necessities of state security.

Safety deposit box 247 contained three items: a leather journal bound with string, a small wooden box carved with symbols that made Dmitri's supernatural senses tingle with recognition, and a letter addressed simply to "My Son."

Dmitri returned to his apartment and spread the contents across his kitchen table, feeling like an archaeologist excavating the buried history of his own life. The letter, written in careful Russian script, began with words that shattered everything he thought he understood about his family:

Dmitri,

If you are reading this, then I am dead and you have reached the age where the weight of our bloodline can no longer be concealed from you. Your mother and I agreed long ago that you should be raised believing your father died a hero's death in service to a noble cause. This was not entirely false—I did serve the Soviet Union, and I did risk my life for what I believed were noble purposes. But the truth is more complicated than heroism, and more dangerous than death.

My name was Anton Volkov, and I carried the same gifts that now manifest in you. The ability to sense and manipulate the fundamental forces that hold matter together, to heal from injuries that should be fatal, to perceive the flow of energy through systems both living and mechanical. These abilities are inherited, passed from generation to generation through bloodlines that stretch back over six centuries.

We are part of something called the Covenant of Shadows, an organization founded by Eleanor Blackthorne in 1348 to protect humanity from the consequences of supernatural revelation. For over six hundred years, our families have hidden their gifts, using them only in secret service to causes that preserve the greater good while maintaining the illusion that such abilities do not exist.

The letter continued for several pages, detailing the history that Dmitri's mother had only hinted at in carefully edited stories. Anton described the original covenant, Eleanor's vision of catastrophic revelation, the centuries of careful concealment that had protected both the gifted and the ungifted from the consequences of supernatural warfare.

But as Dmitri read deeper into his father's account, the tone shifted from explanation to confession:

During the Great Patriotic War, your mother and I faced choices that haunt me still. We discovered Nazi programs designed to weaponize supernatural abilities, facilities where gifted children were being tortured and experimented upon. We had the power to

195

stop these atrocities, to rescue innocent lives, to use our gifts openly in service to obvious moral good.

Instead, we chose secrecy. We allowed the children to die rather than risk exposing the existence of supernatural abilities to a world that we believed was not ready for such knowledge. We told ourselves that we were preserving humanity from a greater catastrophe, that individual sacrifices were necessary to prevent the species-wide disaster that Eleanor had foreseen.

I have spent the forty years since the war's end questioning whether that choice was wisdom or cowardice, whether the covenant's teachings represent accumulated knowledge or accumulated fear. The children who died in those Nazi facilities died because people like us chose preservation of secrets over preservation of lives.

Dmitri set down the letter and reached for the journal, its leather cover worn smooth by decades of handling. The pages contained what appeared to be a detailed history of covenant activities from the perspective of someone who had gradually lost faith in the organization's mission. Anton had documented decades of supernatural intervention in world events, showing how the covenant's attempts to prevent revelation had often caused greater suffering than the revelation itself might have produced.

Most damning was a section dealing with nuclear weapons development. According to Anton's research, several covenant members had been involved in the Manhattan Project, using their abilities to accelerate uranium enrichment and ensure the success of the first atomic bombs. Their justification had been that ending World War II quickly would prevent greater casualties, but the result had been the introduction of weapons that made Eleanor's vision of species extinction seem almost inevitable.

"The covenant teaches that revelation of supernatural abilities would lead to their weaponization by governments," Anton had written in one particularly bitter entry. "But we have been weaponizing ourselves for centuries, serving the very governments we claim to fear, participating in the very conflicts we pretend to prevent. We have become the thing we most feared: supernatural beings in service to mass destruction."

The wooden box contained physical evidence to support Anton's written accusations: photographs of covenant members in Nazi uniforms, Soviet intelligence documents describing supernatural assets, classified American reports about "enhanced individuals" in various government programs. The evidence painted a picture of systematic infiltration and cooperation that made the covenant's claims of independence from governmental control seem laughable.

But the most personal revelation came in the journal's final entries, written in the months before Anton's death:

My son works at Chernobyl, unaware that his abilities make him uniquely qualified to understand the reactor's true condition. I have monitored the plant's operations through contacts in the nuclear industry, and I fear that Dmitri will soon face the same choice that haunted your mother and me during the war: whether to use supernatural gifts to prevent immediate suffering or maintain the secrecy that supposedly protects humanity from greater catastrophe.

I pray that he will be wiser than his parents. I pray that he will find a way to serve both conscience and covenant. But if he cannot, if the choice becomes as stark as ours was, I hope he will remember that some things are worth risking everything to protect.

The covenant has survived for six centuries by teaching each generation that their individual moral judgment is less important than accumulated organizational wisdom. But wisdom that requires the sacrifice of innocent lives may not be wisdom at all. It may simply be fear dressed in the language of necessity.

Dmitri closed the journal and stared at the evidence of his heritage spread across his kitchen table. Everything he had believed about his family, about his obligations, about the nature of the supernatural community that had shaped his hidden life, was revealed to be either incomplete or entirely false.

His father had been alive until three weeks ago—alive and watching while Dmitri struggled with the same impossible choices that had defined the Volkov bloodline for generations. Anton had known about the Chernobyl test, had understood the nuclear crisis his son would face, but had chosen to let Dmitri make his own decision rather than burden him with inherited wisdom that might be corrupted by accumulated guilt.

The irony was overwhelming. While Dmitri had been preventing a nuclear disaster through supernatural intervention, his father had been dying of natural causes, carrying to his grave the weight of all the disasters he had failed to prevent through supernatural inaction.

But perhaps most crushing was the realization that Dmitri's choice to act—his decision to use his abilities to prevent the Chernobyl explosion—represented not just a break with covenant tradition but a direct repudiation of the choice his parents had made during the war. Where they had chosen secrecy over service, preservation of self over protection of innocents, he had chosen to risk everything to prevent suffering.

Whether that choice would prove wise or catastrophic remained to be seen. But as Dmitri sat in his apartment, surrounded by the evidence of six centuries of supernatural secrecy and systematic moral compromise, he felt the weight of inherited responsibility settling on his shoulders like a cloak he could never remove.

His father's shadow stretched across decades of hidden history, touching everything from Nazi genocide to nuclear weapons development to the ongoing question of whether the gifted served humanity better through revelation or concealment. And now that shadow fell across Dmitri's own choices, forcing him to confront the possibility that his intervention at Chernobyl had been either the beginning of a new chapter in covenant history or the first step toward the catastrophic revelation that Eleanor Blackthorne had warned against.

Outside his window, the city of Pripyat slept peacefully, its residents unaware that their continued existence depended on supernatural intervention they could never know about. And in apartments and houses around the world, other children of the gifted were inheriting the same impossible legacy, preparing to face a future where the ancient conflict between secrecy and service would take new forms but never truly end.

The only question was whether Dmitri would have the courage to face the consequences of his choice, or whether he would follow his father's example and spend the rest of his life wondering whether he had been wise or merely afraid.

The weight of history pressed down on him like radioactive fallout, invisible but deadly, contaminating everything it touched with the accumulated guilt of generations who had chosen preservation over action. But unlike radiation, this contamination could not be cleaned up or contained. It could only be carried forward, passed to the next generation, and transformed through choices that would echo through centuries yet to come.

Anton Volkov's shadow was long and dark, but it was no longer the only shadow in the room. Dmitri had cast his own shadow now, and only time would tell whether it would prove longer or shorter than his father's—and whether it would point toward light or deeper darkness.

CHAPTER 17: THE CHOICE AT REACTOR FOUR

Chernobyl Nuclear Power Plant, Ukrainian SSR

April 26, 1986 - 3:47 AM

The radiation alarm that pierced the pre-dawn darkness of Reactor 4 should never have sounded.

Dmitri bolted upright in the plant dormitory, his supernatural senses screaming warnings that had nothing to do with the mechanical shriek of emergency sirens. His intervention during the safety test three hours earlier had prevented the catastrophic steam explosion that would have scattered the reactor core across half of Ukraine, but what he felt now was different—a slower, more insidious failure that his rushed supernatural triage had failed to address completely.

In his haste to prevent immediate catastrophe, Dmitri had focused on dampening the runaway nuclear reaction and preventing the pressure vessel rupture. But the reactor's cooling systems had already been compromised, and without constant supernatural intervention—the kind that would be impossible to hide from his colleagues—the core was still heading toward meltdown.

He dressed quickly and ran toward the reactor building, his enhanced senses painting a detailed picture of the crisis unfolding within the containment structure. The fuel assemblies were overheating despite the successful shutdown, coolant was leaking from damaged primary circuits, and radioactive steam was beginning to vent into areas where maintenance workers were still conducting post-test inspections.

The scene in the reactor building was chaos tempered by Soviet training and discipline. Emergency crews were responding to alarms they didn't fully understand, following procedures designed for scenarios that didn't match the complex reality of partial system failure. Plant Director Bryukhanov was shouting orders while trying to make sense of instrument readings that contradicted each other, some showing normal conditions while others indicated dangerous levels of radiation.

"Dmitri!" Anya's voice cut through the confusion as she spotted him entering the control room. Her face was pale with exhaustion and growing fear. "Thank God you're here. We need every qualified engineer we can get."

"What's the situation?" he asked, though his supernatural awareness already told him everything the instruments couldn't detect.

"Coolant leak in the primary circuit," reported Shift Supervisor Akimov, his voice tight with controlled panic. "Radiation levels in several compartments are climbing beyond safe limits. We have maintenance personnel trapped in areas we can't reach due to contamination."

Dmitri felt the familiar weight of impossible choice settling on his shoulders. His partial intervention had prevented the immediate disaster, but three maintenance workers were now trapped in a section of the reactor building where radiation levels would kill them within hours. The cooling system failure was gradual but inexorable—without supernatural assistance, the reactor core would eventually breach containment and release radioactive material into the atmosphere.

He could save the trapped workers easily enough. A subtle manipulation of radiation fields, a careful reshaping of damaged cooling pipes, a precise adjustment of airflow patterns to clear contaminated areas. But each intervention would leave traces that nuclear engineers would eventually detect and investigate.

"I'm going in," announced Boris Stolyarchuk, a senior engineer whose courage was matched only by his ignorance of the true radiation levels in the affected areas. "If there are men trapped in there—"

"No," Dmitri said sharply, then caught himself. Too forceful, too revealing of knowledge he shouldn't possess. "The radiation levels are too high. We need to assess the situation more carefully before risking additional lives."

But even as he spoke, Dmitri could sense the trapped workers growing weaker, their cellular systems beginning to fail under the assault of ionizing radiation. In perhaps thirty minutes, they would pass the point where even his supernatural healing abilities couldn't save them.

"The dosimeters are malfunctioning," Anya reported, studying instrument readings with growing confusion. "Some are showing normal background levels while others indicate lethal contamination in the same areas."

Of course they were malfunctioning. Dmitri's hasty intervention had created localized radiation anomalies that no instrument was designed to measure. Areas where he had unconsciously absorbed and redirected radioactive energy showed artificially low readings, while sections he hadn't been able to reach displayed the true scope of the contamination.

"I'll check the radiation levels personally," Dmitri decided, knowing that his supernatural senses would provide accurate information regardless of instrumental failure. "If there's a chance to reach the trapped workers—"

"Absolutely not," Anya interrupted, her professional concern overriding any personal feelings. "You're too valuable to risk on a rescue mission that might be impossible anyway."

The irony of her words cut deep. Dmitri was indeed too valuable to risk—not because of his nuclear engineering expertise, but because of supernatural abilities that could prevent or mitigate disasters beyond the comprehension of conventional science. But that value was meaningless if he couldn't use it to save innocent lives.

"Give me ten minutes," he said, moving toward the protective equipment storage. "If I can't reach them safely, I'll retreat immediately."

As Dmitri suited up in radiation protection gear that would be useless against the levels of contamination he was about to face, he made a series of rapid calculations about risk and necessity. The trapped workers would die without intervention. The reactor core would eventually breach containment without constant supernatural monitoring and adjustment. And every minute of delay increased the likelihood that others would be exposed to lethal radiation levels.

His father's journal had spoken of impossible choices between individual lives and species survival. But this felt different—not a choice between revelation and concealment, but a test of whether supernatural abilities could be used responsibly in service to immediate human need.

Dmitri entered the contaminated section of the reactor building with his supernatural senses fully extended, monitoring radiation levels, airflow patterns, and the condition of the trapped workers with precision no instrument could match. The scene that greeted him was a nightmare of twisted metal, escaping steam, and invisible death hanging in the air like a malevolent spirit.

The three maintenance workers—Ivan Kudryavtsev, Valery Perevozchenko, and Anatoly Kurguz—were huddled in a maintenance alcove, their dosimeters shrieking warnings that they had already received potentially lethal doses. But Dmitri's enhanced perception revealed that their condition, while serious, was not yet irreversible.

"Who's there?" Ivan called out weakly as Dmitri approached through the contaminated corridor. "We were told rescue teams couldn't reach us."

"I'm here now," Dmitri replied, his voice muffled by the protective equipment. "Can you walk?"

"Barely," Valery admitted. "The radiation... we can feel it burning us from the inside."

Dmitri could indeed sense the cellular damage the three men had sustained, the DNA breaks and tissue destruction that would prove fatal without intervention. As he helped them to their feet, he made a decision that would haunt him for the rest of his life.

Working quickly and as subtly as possible, Dmitri reached out with his supernatural gift and began repairing the radiation damage at the cellular level. He couldn't heal them completely—that would be too obvious, too miraculous. But he could slow the progression of radiation poisoning, buy them time for conventional medical treatment, give them a chance to survive what should have been a death sentence.

The process required him to absorb much of the radioactive contamination from their bodies into his own, a transfer that would have killed any ordinary person instantly. But Dmitri's gift included an unusual resistance to radiation effects, an ability to process and neutralize radioactive particles that had made him uniquely suited for nuclear engineering work.

"I feel... better," Anatoly said with surprise as they made their way toward the exit. "Stronger than I should."

"Adrenaline," Dmitri lied smoothly. "It can mask radiation symptoms temporarily. We need to get you to medical immediately."

The evacuation proceeded smoothly until they reached the decontamination station, where Dmitri's own radiation exposure became apparent. The dosimeter readings were impossible—levels that should have killed him ten times over, absorbed in the few minutes he had spent in the contaminated area.

"Something's wrong with the equipment," the medical technician announced, studying readings that defied every principle of radiation safety. "No one could survive exposure at these levels."

"Equipment malfunction," Dmitri agreed, though he could feel Anya's sharp gaze studying him with growing suspicion. "The same problems affecting the reactor monitors are probably affecting the dosimeters."

But his explanation sounded hollow even to his own ears. Too many instruments were showing impossible readings, too many systems were displaying anomalous behavior that coincidentally benefited the plant's emergency response efforts. To someone with Anya's analytical mind, the pattern would soon become obvious.

As the three rescued workers were transported to medical facilities for treatment they no longer desperately needed, Dmitri found himself facing questions he couldn't answer honestly. How had he known exactly where to find the trapped men? How had he navigated the contaminated areas with such precision? And most importantly, how had he survived radiation exposure that should have killed him within minutes?

"Your dosimeter readings are still climbing," Anya observed as they stood in the decontamination area, watching technicians struggle with equipment that couldn't process the supernatural traces of Dmitri's intervention. "You should be showing symptoms of acute radiation syndrome by now."

"I feel fine," Dmitri replied, which was true. His supernatural gift had not only protected him from radiation effects but had actually grown stronger through exposure to the intense energy fields within the reactor building. He felt more alert, more capable, more connected to the atomic forces that sustained both nuclear reactors and living organisms.

"That's impossible," Anya said flatly. "The readings indicate lethal exposure. You should be vomiting, experiencing cellular breakdown, showing signs of imminent system failure."

Instead, Dmitri looked healthier than he had in months, his skin showing the subtle glow that marked someone whose supernatural abilities had been recently exercised to their full potential. To trained eyes like Anya's, accustomed to observing the effects of radiation on human physiology, his condition would appear miraculous.

"Perhaps the equipment really is malfunctioning," Dmitri suggested weakly.

"Or perhaps," Anya said quietly, her voice carrying a note of scientific fascination mixed with growing unease, "there are factors affecting this situation that we don't understand."

As dawn broke over the Chernobyl facility, painting the reactor buildings in shades of gold and red that seemed ominous rather than beautiful, Dmitri realized that his choice to intervene had accomplished its immediate goal while creating longer-term problems that might prove impossible to solve.

The three maintenance workers would survive with minimal long-term effects. The reactor core was stable, its meltdown prevented through careful supernatural intervention that would be difficult to detect or explain. The immediate crisis had been resolved through the application of abilities that no human being should possess.

But Anya was asking questions that had no conventional answers. Medical personnel were documenting exposure levels that defied known science. And somewhere in the chain of investigation and reporting that would follow any nuclear incident, people with the resources and intelligence to recognize patterns would begin to notice that the Chernobyl crisis had been resolved through means that transcended ordinary engineering expertise.

Dmitri Petrov had saved lives and prevented disaster through the careful application of supernatural gifts. But in doing so, he had also taken the first steps down a path that would eventually lead to the revelation his family had spent generations trying to prevent.

The choice at Reactor Four was complete. Now came the far more difficult task of living with its consequences.

CHAPTER 18: LIVING WITH GHOSTS

Moscow, Russian SFSR

October 1987

The official report on the Chernobyl incident was a masterpiece of bureaucratic fiction, transforming a near-catastrophe into a testament to Soviet engineering excellence and the heroic response of nuclear facility personnel. Dmitri read through the classified version—the one that acknowledged the severity of what had almost occurred—while sitting in a sterile office deep within the Ministry of Energy's Moscow headquarters.

According to the report, the safety test had proceeded exactly as planned. Reactor 4 had been successfully shut down without incident. The minor radiation leaks that occurred during post-test maintenance were attributed to equipment fatigue and had been contained through standard emergency procedures. The three workers who had been briefly trapped in contaminated areas had recovered completely, showing no long-term effects from their minimal exposure.

Every word was technically accurate. Every conclusion was completely false.

"Your analysis of the reactor's performance during the test was particularly insightful," commented Dr. Yevgeny Velikhov, the nuclear physicist who had been appointed to review the incident for the Academy of Sciences. "Your recommendations for cooling system improvements could prevent similar problems in the future."

Dmitri nodded politely, though the praise felt like ashes in his mouth. His recommendations were based on supernatural knowledge of atomic processes that no human instrument could detect, insights gained through abilities that would see him imprisoned or worse if their existence were ever discovered. He was being celebrated for preventing a disaster that his own intervention had made possible to prevent.

"There is one aspect of the incident that remains... puzzling," Dr. Velikhov continued, studying a file that Dmitri couldn't see. "The radiation exposure data for several personnel involved in the emergency response. The readings are inconsistent with known models of radiation dispersal and human physiological response."

"Equipment malfunction was widespread that night," Dmitri replied carefully. "The electromagnetic effects from the reactor shutdown may have interfered with dosimeter accuracy."

"Perhaps. Although some of the readings are so anomalous that they suggest either complete instrument failure or..." Dr. Velikhov paused, studying Dmitri's face with the intensity of someone accustomed to detecting deception. "Or the presence of factors that our current understanding of radiation physics cannot account for."

The conversation ended with polite professional courtesy, but Dmitri left the ministry building with the certain knowledge that his intervention at Chernobyl had created questions that would never be fully answered or completely forgotten. The Soviet system might classify and bury inconvenient truths, but individual scientists like Velikhov would continue to puzzle over anomalies that challenged their understanding of natural law.

The train journey back to Pripyat gave Dmitri time to think about the life he was returning to—a life increasingly defined by the weight of secrets and the strain of relationships built on fundamental deceptions. Anya had grown distant since the incident, her scientific mind unable to reconcile Dmitri's impossible survival with any rational explanation. Their conversations had become careful, professional, marked by the sort of polite restraint that characterized interactions between people who no longer trusted each other completely.

He found her that evening in the plant's technical library, surrounded by radiation safety manuals and medical journals, pursuing research that Dmitri suspected was focused on understanding his survival rather than improving general safety protocols.

"Working late again?" he asked, settling into the chair across from her desk.

"Trying to understand something that doesn't seem to have a rational explanation," Anya replied without looking up from the journal she was reading. "Did you know that there have been seventeen documented cases in the past century of individuals surviving radiation exposure that should have been immediately fatal?"

Dmitri felt his blood turn cold. "Equipment malfunction is more common than people realize—"

"Not equipment malfunction," Anya interrupted, finally meeting his eyes. "Cases where multiple independent measurements confirmed lethal exposure levels, but the subjects showed no symptoms of radiation poisoning. No cellular damage. No immune system suppression. No long-term health effects."

She turned the journal around so Dmitri could see the article she had been reading—a medical paper from 1945 describing the survival of a Nagasaki physician who had been less than a kilometer from ground zero when the atomic bomb detonated. The man had not only survived but had continued treating patients for weeks afterward, showing no signs of radiation sickness despite calculated exposure levels that should have killed him within hours.

"Dr. Takashi Nagai," Anya continued. "He attributed his survival to divine intervention and spent the rest of his life promoting nuclear disarmament. But the medical evidence suggests something else entirely—some form of natural radiation resistance that current science cannot explain."

Dmitri scanned the article while his mind raced through the implications. Seventeen documented cases over a century suggested that other members of his supernatural bloodline had found themselves in situations where their abilities had been exposed to scientific scrutiny. The pattern Anya was detecting wasn't unique to Chernobyl—it was evidence of a global phenomenon that the covenant had somehow managed to suppress or explain away for generations.

"What do you think explains these cases?" he asked, though he dreaded the answer.

"I don't know," Anya admitted. "But I'm beginning to suspect that our understanding of human physiology is less complete than we assumed. That there might be genetic variations, evolutionary adaptations, or..." She paused, clearly struggling with concepts that challenged everything she had been taught about the limits of human capability. "Or abilities that we simply haven't recognized because they manifest so rarely."

The conversation that followed was the most difficult of Dmitri's life. Anya's questions were precise, informed, and focused on exactly the aspects of his survival that he could never explain honestly. She had documented the radiation levels in the contaminated areas, calculated the exposure he must have received, and compared his lack of symptoms to established medical literature about radiation poisoning.

"I know you're hiding something," she said finally, her voice carrying a mixture of frustration and concern. "The question is whether you're protecting yourself or protecting me."

"What do you mean?"

"If you have some form of natural radiation resistance—if you're part of a population that has adapted to survive nuclear exposure—then there are people who would want to study you, understand how that resistance works, potentially use that knowledge for military applications." Anya's expression was troubled. "But if I'm right about what I think I'm observing, then your survival at Chernobyl wasn't luck or equipment malfunction. It was evidence of abilities that could change our understanding of human potential."

Dmitri stared at the woman he loved, realizing that her brilliant mind had carried her to the edge of a truth that would destroy both their lives if she decided to pursue it. Anya was offering him a choice: share his secrets and trust her with knowledge that could expose the entire supernatural community, or continue lying and watch their relationship slowly deteriorate under the weight of unexplained mysteries.

"Some questions are too dangerous to answer," he said quietly.

"Dangerous for whom?"

"For everyone."

That night, alone in his apartment while Anya processed his refusal to explain the impossible, Dmitri opened his father's journal and began reading sections he had previously avoided—detailed accounts of other covenant members who had faced similar moments of potential exposure.

What he found was a catalog of preventable tragedies that stretched back over a century, each one involving gifted individuals who had chosen secrecy over service when their intervention could have saved countless lives.

RMS Titanic, April 14, 1912:

Margaret Ashford (descendant of Matthias, memory manipulation abilities) was traveling first class under the identity of Margaret Brown. During the collision with the iceberg, she could have used her gift to calm the panic that led to lifeboats being launched half-empty, to organize efficient evacuation procedures, to prevent the chaos that cost hundreds of lives. Instead, she maintained her false identity and escaped in one of the first boats, watching from safety as people died in situations her abilities could have prevented.

The official inquiry into the disaster focused on inadequate lifeboat capacity and crew training failures. It never considered how many lives might have been saved by supernatural intervention in the crucial hours after impact.

San Francisco Earthquake, April 18, 1906:

James Delacroix (descendant of Marie, weather manipulation abilities) was working as a meteorologist for the U.S. Weather Bureau when the earthquake struck. His gift could have predicted the disaster days in advance, allowing for evacuation of the most vulnerable areas. In the aftermath, he could have controlled the winds that spread the fires throughout the city, preventing much of the destruction that followed the initial quake.

Instead, he filed routine weather reports that made no mention of the impending catastrophe and fled the city before the extent of the damage became clear. The fires that consumed San Francisco raged for three days, destroying 28,000 buildings and leaving 250,000 people homeless—casualties that could have been drastically reduced by intervention he was capable of providing but chose not to use.

Spanish Influenza Pandemic, 1918-1920:

Elena Torriani (descendant of Giovanni, healing abilities) was serving as a Red Cross nurse in Boston when the pandemic reached its peak. Her gift could have cured patients faster than the disease could spread, broken transmission chains in crowded immigrant neighborhoods, prevented the viral mutations that made successive waves more deadly.

She treated patients with conventional medical techniques while watching them die from a disease she could have stopped with a touch. The pandemic ultimately killed between 50 and 100 million people worldwide—more than the entire Great War that preceded it.

Elena survived to write detailed journals about the moral burden of possessing healing abilities while allowing mass death to occur, but she never wavered in her commitment to covenant secrecy.

Page after page documented similar choices: gifted individuals who had chosen preservation of supernatural secrecy over prevention of human suffering. The pattern was consistent across cultures, time periods, and types of disasters. When faced with the choice between revelation and catastrophe, the covenant's members had consistently chosen to allow catastrophe.

The weight of inherited guilt pressed down on Dmitri like radioactive fallout, contaminating everything he touched with the accumulated moral failures of generations. His father had carried this knowledge for decades, watching his son grow up with abilities that could prevent disasters while knowing that family tradition demanded those abilities remain hidden regardless of the cost in human lives.

But there was something else in Anton's journal, a pattern that became clear only when viewed across the full scope of covenant history. The disasters that had been allowed to occur were not random tragedies—they were increasingly catastrophic events that shaped global politics, economics, and scientific development in ways that served the covenant's long-term interests.

The Titanic disaster had led to international maritime safety regulations that made it easier to track and monitor global shipping. The San Francisco earthquake had justified federal emergency management systems that brought local disasters under central government control. The Spanish flu pandemic had established international health monitoring networks that could identify and track unusual disease patterns—including the genetic markers that indicated supernatural bloodlines.

Each disaster that the covenant had allowed to unfold had ultimately strengthened the governmental systems that made it easier to maintain supernatural secrecy on a global scale. The organization had not simply failed to prevent tragedies—it had allowed them to occur because they served organizational purposes.

The revelation was staggering in its implications. The covenant was not just a conspiracy to hide supernatural abilities from the world— it was a conspiracy that used human suffering as a tool for social engineering, allowing disasters to occur when they advanced the goal of maintaining secrecy and preventing revelation.

As Dmitri closed his father's journal and stared out at the lights of Pripyat, where families slept peacefully in their beds because his supernatural intervention had prevented a nuclear catastrophe, he realized that his choice to act had represented more than just a break with family tradition. It had been a direct repudiation of a system that treated human life as expendable in service to organizational preservation.

The covenant had spent six centuries teaching its members that individual moral judgment was less important than collective survival. But what if collective survival had become indistinguishable from collective moral corruption? What if the organization meant to protect humanity had become humanity's greatest threat?

Tomorrow would bring new questions from Anya, new investigations from Soviet authorities, new challenges to the secrecy that had defined his family for generations. The choice he had made at Reactor Four had saved lives in the immediate term, but it had also set in motion a process that would eventually force a reckoning between the covenant's ancient commitments and the moral demands of the modern world.

Dmitri Petrov lived with ghosts—the ghosts of children who had died in Nazi experiments while his parents chose secrecy over rescue, the ghosts of Titanic passengers who had drowned while covenant members chose concealment over assistance, the ghosts of plague victims who had suffered while healers chose tradition over treatment.

But for the first time in the covenant's long history, those ghosts had been joined by the spirits of people who had lived—reactor workers saved by supernatural intervention, families who would never know how close they had come to radioactive death, children who would grow up healthy because someone had finally chosen service over secrecy.

Whether that choice would prove wise or catastrophic remained to be seen. But as Dmitri prepared for sleep in a world that continued to exist because he had chosen to act rather than obey inherited wisdom, he felt something that his ancestors had perhaps never experienced: the peace that came from knowing he had served conscience over covenant, humanity over heritage.

The ghosts that haunted him now were the spirits of the saved rather than the sacrificed. And for the first time in six centuries of supernatural secrecy, that felt like a burden worth carrying.

CHAPTER 19: DIGITAL AWAKENING

San Francisco, California

March 15, 2020

Maya Chen's supernatural abilities first manifested during a software engineering interview at a startup in SOMA, triggered by the stress of technical questions she couldn't answer and the desperate need to prove herself worthy of a job that would let her escape her family's suffocating expectations.

The interviewer had pulled up a debugging challenge on his laptop—a piece of broken code that senior developers typically spent hours analyzing. Maya stared at the screen, feeling her anxiety spike as the silence stretched beyond comfortable limits, and suddenly the laptop's internal processes became as visible to her consciousness as if she were looking at an anatomical diagram.

She could see the data flows like rivers of light, trace the execution paths through the processor's architecture, follow individual electrons as they moved through circuits that had become extensions of her own nervous system. The broken code wasn't just text on a screen—it was a living system whose disease she could diagnose and heal with the same intuitive understanding that a healer might bring to a patient's wound.

"Found it," Maya said, her fingers moving across the keyboard with impossible speed and precision. "Buffer overflow in the authentication module. Someone forgot to validate input length before passing it to the legacy C library."

The fix took her thirty seconds. The interviewer spent the next ten minutes staring at the corrected code, trying to understand how someone had identified and resolved a bug that had stumped his entire development team for the past week.

"How did you know where to look?" he asked finally.

Maya opened her mouth to explain her debugging process, then realized she didn't actually remember typing the solution. The fix had emerged from some deeper level of consciousness, as if the laptop itself had whispered the answer directly into her mind.

"Lucky guess," she said weakly, though even as she spoke the words, Maya could feel the lie settling into her chest like a tumor that would grow and metastasize until it consumed everything honest about her life.

That had been three months ago. Now, sitting in her small apartment in the Mission District while San Francisco shelter-in-place orders kept the city locked down against a pandemic that had transformed 2020 into a year of global isolation, Maya was learning that her supernatural abilities grew stronger with every day of quarantine-induced digital dependency.

Her laptop sat open on the coffee table, its screen displaying a dozen windows that represented only a fraction of the systems her consciousness was currently inhabiting. She could feel the pulse of the building's WiFi network, sense the flow of data through fiber optic cables that stretched across the city, monitor the endless stream of communications that connected millions of people through devices they had no idea were accessible to someone with her gifts.

The technopathy had evolved far beyond simple debugging. Maya could now interface directly with any electronic system within her range, from smartphones to security cameras to the traffic management grid that controlled every stoplight in the Bay Area. She was becoming a digital ghost, present in every connected device, watching the city's electronic nervous system with awareness that transcended anything the original designers had intended.

It was intoxicating. It was terrifying. And it was completely impossible to hide.

The doorbell chimed through her building's intercom system, though Maya had sensed the visitor's approach long before they reached her apartment. The delivery driver's smartphone had announced his presence the moment he entered her neighborhood, and the GPS tracking data had painted a clear picture of his route from the restaurant to her front door.

"Contactless delivery," the driver announced through the intercom, though Maya could see through his phone's camera that he was wearing a mask and gloves as protection against viral transmission. The pandemic had made human contact suspicious and dangerous, but it had also made digital interaction essential and ubiquitous.

Maya collected her food while her consciousness continued to explore the vast network of connected devices that surrounded her apartment building. Her neighbors' smartphones told stories of quarantine boredom—endless social media scrolling, video streaming, online shopping, digital connections that had become the primary means of human interaction in a world where physical proximity carried the risk of infection.

But there was something else in the digital noise, a pattern that her enhanced awareness had begun to detect over the past few weeks. Certain devices carried traces of unusual activity—data flows that didn't match normal usage patterns, communications that were encrypted beyond standard security protocols, access logs that suggested someone was using technology in ways that transcended conventional human-computer interaction.

Maya was not the only one with supernatural abilities that manifested through digital systems.

The realization had been building for weeks, but tonight it crystallized into certainty as her technopathic senses detected something that made her blood run cold: her own apartment building's security system was being accessed by someone who wasn't using any of the building's authorized devices.

She felt the intrusion like a physical presence, a consciousness that moved through the building's network with the same fluid awareness that she brought to digital exploration. Whoever was accessing the system had abilities similar to her own, but their touch felt older, more experienced, carrying traces of techniques that had been refined over years or perhaps decades of practice.

Maya isolated her laptop from the building's WiFi and switched to a cellular connection that she immediately began encrypting through layers of tunneling protocols. If someone was hunting technopaths through digital networks, she needed to make herself as invisible as possible while she figured out whether the presence she had detected was friend or foe.

Her phone buzzed with a text message from an unknown number: "We need to talk. You're not safe using unprotected networks. Basement laundry room in ten minutes."

Maya stared at the message while her enhanced senses probed her phone's communication logs. The text had been delivered through normal cellular channels, but the sender's identity was hidden behind encryption that would have required government-level resources to penetrate. Whoever was contacting her had both supernatural abilities and access to sophisticated security technology.

Every instinct screamed at her to ignore the message, to pack her essentials and disappear into the digital underground where her technopathy could keep her hidden indefinitely. But the part of her mind that had been raised on science fiction and fantasy novels was desperate to finally meet someone who could explain what was happening to her, who could tell her whether she was losing her sanity or gaining abilities that should not exist.

Ten minutes later, Maya descended to her building's basement with her laptop bag slung over her shoulder and her consciousness extended through every connected device in the vicinity. The laundry room was empty except for a young man about her own age, sitting on one of the folding tables with a tablet in his lap and an expression that mixed wariness with desperate hope.

"You're the one who's been accessing the building systems," Maya said. It wasn't a question.

"And you're the one who's been practicing on the traffic lights," he replied. "I'm Lucas. Lucas Blackthorne."

The surname hit Maya like an electric shock. Blackthorne—the same family name that appeared in the fragmentary historical documents her grandmother had shown her, stories about supernatural abilities that ran in bloodlines and ancient obligations that demanded secrecy above all else.

"Your family..." Maya began.

"Founded the organization that your family probably told you to avoid," Lucas finished. "Though 'founded' might be too generous a term. 'Corrupted over six centuries' would be more accurate."

Lucas gestured to his tablet, which displayed what appeared to be a secure communication interface connecting dozens of users across the globe. "There are others like us. More than you might expect, but fewer than there should be given the size of the population that carries supernatural genes."

Maya approached cautiously, her technopathic senses probing the tablet's security protocols. What she found was impressive—military-grade encryption wrapped around communication software that had been designed specifically for users with enhanced digital capabilities.

"How many others?" she asked.

"Active members of this network? Maybe fifty worldwide. But our demographic analysis suggests there should be thousands of people with manifesting abilities, possibly tens of thousands if you include minor gifts that might not be immediately obvious."

"So where are they?"

Lucas's expression darkened. "Dead, mostly. Or hiding so deep that they might as well be dead. The organization my ancestor founded—

the Covenant of Shadows—has spent the past six hundred years systematically suppressing supernatural abilities through a combination of selective breeding, strategic elimination, and psychological conditioning that teaches gifted individuals to fear their own power."

Maya felt the familiar weight of inherited secrets settling on her shoulders. Her grandmother's stories had always emphasized the dangers of revealing supernatural abilities, the catastrophic consequences that would follow if the world learned that people with impossible powers lived among them. But Lucas was suggesting that the real danger came not from revelation but from the organization that enforced concealment.

"Why contact me now?" she asked.

"Because the covenant is losing control," Lucas replied, gesturing toward the tablet's interface. "Digital technology has made it impossible to maintain the kind of comprehensive secrecy that they've relied on for centuries. Every time someone like you uses technopathy, every time someone like me has a prophetic vision that prevents a disaster, every time any of us exercises our abilities in a world filled with surveillance cameras and data logging systems, we create evidence that can be detected and analyzed."

Maya thought about her own experiences over the past few months—the debugging session that had been too fast and too intuitive, the traffic lights that had changed in her favor too consistently, the WiFi networks that had started responding to her presence before she consciously tried to access them. Each incident had left digital traces that a sufficiently motivated investigator could follow back to their source.

"They know about us," she realized.

"Multiple government agencies, several private organizations, at least three different academic research programs," Lucas confirmed. "The question isn't whether supernatural abilities will be revealed to the public—it's whether that revelation will be controlled by us or by people who want to study us like laboratory animals."

Maya studied the communication interface on Lucas's tablet, watching encrypted messages flow between users whose screen names suggested they were scattered across every continent. The network represented something unprecedented in the covenant's history: a global community of the gifted who were choosing connection over concealment, collaboration over secrecy.

"What does your prophecy tell you about how this ends?" she asked.

Lucas's smile was grim. "That's the problem. My visions have been showing multiple possible futures, all of them involving some form of supernatural revelation within the next five years. But the details change depending on the choices we make. Some timelines show controlled disclosure that leads to integration and cooperation. Others show exposure through investigation and exploitation that leads to supernatural warfare."

"And the covenant?"

"Wants to prevent revelation at any cost, even if that cost includes eliminating every gifted individual on the planet." Lucas closed his tablet and met Maya's eyes with an expression that mixed determination with desperation. "We think they've already started. Unexplained deaths, disappearances, accidents that happen to people whose digital footprints suggest supernatural activity. The pattern became obvious once we started sharing information."

Maya felt the world shifting around her as she processed the implications of what Lucas was telling her. Everything her family had taught her about the covenant—that it existed to protect the gifted from persecution by ordinary humans—was apparently false. The real threat came from within the supernatural community itself, from an organization that had become so focused on maintaining secrecy that it was willing to commit genocide to preserve organizational control.

"So what do we do?" she asked.

"We build an alternative," Lucas replied. "A network that can coordinate global revelation on our terms, with safeguards in place to prevent the catastrophic outcomes that the covenant fears. We use our abilities to help humanity adapt to the knowledge that we exist, rather than hiding from that knowledge until it's discovered by people who want to exploit us."

Maya looked around the laundry room where they were meeting—a basement space in a city locked down by a pandemic, surrounded by washing machines and dryers that represented the most mundane aspects of human existence. It seemed like an unlikely place to plan a revolution that would reshape humanity's understanding of what was possible.

But as she extended her consciousness through the building's network and felt the pulse of digital systems that connected her to billions of other human beings around the world, Maya realized that the revolution had already begun. Every smartphone, every WiFi network, every connected device was a potential gateway for someone with her abilities. The infrastructure that the covenant had always feared—the technology that could expose supernatural abilities to global scrutiny—was also the tool that could make revelation manageable and beneficial rather than catastrophic.

"I'm in," she said, accepting Lucas's invitation to join a conspiracy that would either save or doom everyone who carried supernatural gifts in their blood.

As Maya uploaded her consciousness into the encrypted network that connected gifted individuals across the globe, she felt the familiar electric thrill of discovering new systems to explore and master. But this time, the system she was joining was not a collection of devices and databases—it was a community of people who had chosen to embrace their true nature rather than hide from it.

The digital awakening that had begun in a software engineering interview three months earlier was about to become something much larger: the beginning of the end of six centuries of supernatural secrecy, and the start of a new chapter in the relationship between the gifted and the world they were meant to protect.

Whether that new chapter would be written in cooperation or conflict remained to be seen. But for the first time in her life, Maya Chen was not facing the burden of her abilities alone.

CHAPTER 20: PROPHETIC INHERITANCE

Boston, Massachusetts

June 21, 2020

The vision hit Lucas Blackthorne during a routine morning jog through Boston Common, striking with the sudden violence that had characterized his prophetic episodes since childhood. One moment he was running past the bronze statue of George Washington, his mind focused on pandemic-adjusted exercise routines and the encrypted messages he'd received overnight from Maya's growing network. The next, reality fractured around him like glass struck by a hammer.

But this vision was different from the catastrophic revelations that had shaped six centuries of covenant doctrine. Instead of seeing supernatural abilities exposed to public knowledge leading to warfare and extinction, Lucas found himself witnessing a world where the gifted had become so committed to concealment that they had turned their powers inward, consuming themselves in an orgy of supernatural violence that made Eleanor's original prophecy seem merciful by comparison.

He saw covenant members hunting their own children, eliminating anyone whose abilities manifested too strongly or too publicly. He watched as the organization's leadership implemented systematic sterilization programs to gradually reduce the population of the gifted to more "manageable" levels. Most horrifying of all, he witnessed the covenant's final solution: a biological weapon designed to target supernatural bloodlines specifically, deployed by members who had concluded that the only way to prevent revelation was to eliminate every trace of supernatural genetics from the human population.

The vision ended with the same empty settlement that had haunted Eleanor's original prophecy—but this time, it was empty not because humanity had destroyed itself fighting the gifted, but because the gifted had destroyed themselves to preserve a secret that no longer mattered.

Lucas collapsed on a park bench, his body shaking from the psychic shock of experiencing mass extinction from a completely different causal chain than anything in his family's historical records. For over six hundred years, the Blackthorne bloodline had carried Eleanor's vision of revelation-induced catastrophe as absolute truth, the foundation upon which every moral choice and strategic decision had been built.

But what Lucas had just experienced suggested that Eleanor's vision was incomplete—or worse, deliberately edited to conceal alternatives that might have led to different choices by subsequent generations.

That evening, Lucas made his way to the climate-controlled storage facility in Cambridge where his family maintained their most sensitive historical documents. The Blackthorne archives were more extensive than those of most covenant families, preserved through a combination of academic connections and private wealth that had allowed them to maintain detailed records across centuries of political upheaval and social change.

What Lucas sought was not in the carefully catalogued main collection, but in a section of documents that had been sealed by his grandfather with instructions that they only be opened by someone with "sufficient strength of vision to bear the weight of complete truth." Lucas had always assumed this referred to the psychological burden of understanding humanity's potential for supernatural warfare. Now he suspected it meant something entirely different.

The sealed documents were contained in a lead-lined box that required both a physical key and a DNA sample to open. Inside, Lucas found materials that had been hidden from covenant leadership for over six centuries: Eleanor Blackthorne's complete prophetic journals, including visions that had never been shared with Augustine or any of the other original covenant members.

The first journal contained familiar material—detailed descriptions of the revelation catastrophe that had justified the covenant's creation, accounts of supernatural abilities being weaponized by governments and turned against the ungifted population. But the second journal painted a very different picture of humanity's potential futures.

"I have seen the other path," Eleanor had written in careful medieval script, *"the future that unfolds when the gifted choose perfect*

concealment over imperfect revelation. It is no less terrible than the first vision, though its terrors take different forms."

What followed was a meticulous description of exactly the kind of future Lucas had experienced in his morning vision. Eleanor had foreseen that prolonged secrecy would eventually corrupt the covenant itself, transforming it from protector of the gifted into their greatest threat. She had seen the psychological damage that would accumulate across generations forced to live as shadows, the inevitable paranoia that would lead to internal persecution, and the final genocide that would be carried out not by fearful humans but by guilt-ridden supernatural beings who had lost all sense of their original purpose.

"The revelation path leads to war between the gifted and ungifted, ending in mutual destruction within a single generation," Eleanor had written. "The concealment path leads to war within the gifted themselves, ending in self-destruction across multiple generations. Both paths lead to the empty settlement, to silence where humanity should sing."

Lucas read through the night, his understanding of covenant history crumbling with each page. Eleanor had not founded the organization because she believed concealment was the only way to prevent catastrophe—she had founded it because she believed it was the less immediately dangerous of two equally catastrophic alternatives. The covenant was not meant to be a permanent solution, but a temporary measure that would buy time for a third option to emerge.

"I have chosen to share only the revelation vision with Augustine and the others," Eleanor had written in what appeared to be one of her final entries. "If they understood that concealment also leads to destruction, they might choose revelation as the lesser evil, triggering the immediate catastrophe I have seen. Better that they commit themselves fully to the path of secrecy, believing it to be the path of salvation, than that they choose poorly between two forms of damnation."

"But I record the complete truth here for my descendants, trusting that future generations will possess the wisdom to find the third path that my limited sight cannot perceive. The gifted must neither reveal themselves completely nor conceal themselves perfectly. They must find a balance that allows them to exist authentically while preventing the catastrophic polarization that destroys both visions' worlds."

"When the time comes—and my prophetic gift tells me it will come within seven centuries of this writing—my blood will know the truth and act upon it. The choice between revelation and concealment will be revealed as false, and the real choice will finally become clear."

Lucas set down the journal and stared at the storage facility's concrete walls, feeling the weight of inherited deception settling on his shoulders like lead. For over six hundred years, the covenant had made decisions based on deliberately incomplete information. Every moral struggle, every impossible choice, every tragedy that had resulted from choosing secrecy over service had been based on the false premise that concealment was the path of preservation rather than simply a different route to the same ultimate destruction.

Eleanor had not been a visionary leader guiding humanity away from catastrophe—she had been a woman trapped between two equally horrible futures, choosing to lie to her followers about the true scope of the choice they faced rather than risk them making the wrong decision with complete information.

The implications were staggering. Matthias Ashford's moral agony during the Salem witch trials, Anton and Greta's impossible choice during World War II, Dmitri's decision to break with tradition at Chernobyl—all of it had been shaped by a fundamental misunderstanding about the nature of the choice they faced. They had believed they were choosing between salvation and damnation, when in reality they were choosing between different forms of damnation while remaining ignorant of the possibility of salvation.

Lucas reached for his encrypted phone and began composing a message to Maya and the other members of their growing network. What he had to tell them would shatter the ideological foundation of supernatural society, calling into question not just the covenant's methods but the entire framework of assumptions that had governed the gifted for over six centuries.

But as he began to type, Lucas hesitated. Eleanor had faced this same choice—whether to share complete information and risk catastrophic decision-making, or to maintain partial secrecy and guide choices toward what she hoped would be a better outcome. She had chosen deception, and that choice had led to six centuries of suffering and moral corruption within the supernatural community.

What would happen if Lucas made the opposite choice? If he shared Eleanor's complete vision with people who were already questioning the covenant's authority and considering the possibility of controlled revelation? Would they make better decisions with more complete information, or would the knowledge that both revelation and concealment led to destruction push them toward desperate choices that accelerated the very catastrophes Eleanor had tried to prevent?

Lucas stared at his phone's screen, cursor blinking after a few words of introduction, while the weight of prophetic inheritance pressed down on him like the accumulated guilt of twenty-seven generations. He was holding information that could either save or doom the supernatural community, and the choice of whether to share it would determine whether his generation would finally break the cycle of deception that had defined the covenant since its creation.

Outside the storage facility, Boston slept through another night of pandemic uncertainty, while around the world other descendants of Eleanor's original conspiracy wrestled with their own impossible choices about revelation and concealment. The information Lucas had discovered would change everything—if he chose to share it.

But first, he needed to understand what Eleanor's "third path" might look like in practice. The founder of the covenant had been operating in the fourteenth century, limited by the technology and social structures of her time. The gifted of 2020 had tools and opportunities that Eleanor could never have imagined—global communication networks, scientific understanding of genetics and psychology, political systems that at least theoretically valued individual rights and diversity.

Perhaps the third path Eleanor had been unable to envision was finally becoming possible. Perhaps the choice between revelation and concealment really was false, and there was a way for the gifted to exist authentically without triggering either catastrophic outcome.

But finding that path would require abandoning six centuries of accumulated wisdom—or accumulated fear—and trusting that a generation raised on partial truths could handle complete information better than their ancestors had.

Lucas closed the journal and sat back in the storage facility's fluorescent lighting, feeling like an archaeologist who had discovered that everything he thought he knew about ancient history was based on deliberately falsified evidence. The prophetic inheritance he had received was not just the ability to see possible futures, but the burden of deciding which truths were safe to share and which were too dangerous for his community to handle.

It was the same burden Eleanor had carried, and the same choice that had led to six centuries of systematic deception and moral compromise. The question was whether Lucas would have the courage to break that cycle, even if doing so risked triggering the very catastrophes his ancestor had tried so desperately to prevent.

As he prepared to leave the storage facility with Eleanor's hidden journals in his possession, Lucas realized that he was about to become either the salvation or the destruction of everything the covenant had worked to preserve. The choice he made about sharing Eleanor's complete vision would echo through every future timeline he could perceive, determining whether the gifted finally found their third path or simply accelerated their journey toward the empty settlement that haunted both of Eleanor's prophecies.

The weight of history had never felt heavier, but for the first time in his life, Lucas understood that it was a weight he did not have to carry alone.

CHAPTER 21: THE GLOBAL NETWORK

San Francisco, California

September 12, 2020

Maya Chen's consciousness stretched across six continents simultaneously, her technopathic awareness flowing through fiber optic cables, satellite links, and cellular networks to touch the minds of gifted individuals who had never imagined they might not be alone. From her apartment overlooking the fog-shrouded Golden Gate Bridge, she was orchestrating the largest gathering of supernatural abilities in human history—all of it taking place in cyberspace, invisible to the governments and organizations that were finally beginning to notice patterns they couldn't explain.

The secure communication network she had built over the past six months was a masterpiece of distributed encryption and supernatural enhancement. Each node was hosted on servers owned by tech companies whose systems Maya could access without leaving traces, while the routing protocols she had designed made the network traffic indistinguishable from ordinary business communications. To outside observers, the hundreds of gifted individuals connecting through her system appeared to be engaged in perfectly normal video conferences and file sharing.

But to Maya's enhanced perception, the network pulsed with the golden threads that marked supernatural consciousness, creating a web of connection that spanned the globe like a vast nervous system awakening to its own existence.

"Connection established with Node 47," Maya announced to Lucas, who sat at her kitchen table surrounded by laptops displaying real-time feeds from gifted individuals across the world. "That's Dr. Yuki Tanaka in Kyoto. She's a molecular biologist with the ability to manipulate cellular structures at the genetic level."

Lucas barely looked up from the prophetic visions that had been flowing through his consciousness with increasing intensity over the past month. Since discovering Eleanor's hidden journals, his gift had evolved from occasional glimpses of possible futures to a constant stream of interconnected timelines that branched and merged like rivers in a vast delta. The weight of seeing all possible outcomes simultaneously was taking its toll—dark circles under his eyes, hands that shook slightly when he wasn't concentrating, the pale complexion of someone whose consciousness spent more time in the future than the present.

"The accelerating manifestations are confirmed," he said, studying data that Maya's network had been collecting from gifted individuals worldwide. "In the past six months, we've documented more new ability emergences than occurred in the previous five years combined."

Maya nodded grimly. The pattern was undeniable—supernatural abilities were awakening in people who had shown no previous signs of being gifted, while those who already possessed abilities reported significant increases in power and range. The carefully maintained balance that had allowed the covenant to hide small numbers of mildly gifted individuals was breaking down as more people developed abilities that were impossible to conceal.

"Theory?" Maya asked, though she suspected she already knew the answer.

"Collective awakening triggered by global stress," Lucas replied. "The pandemic, economic uncertainty, political upheaval, environmental catastrophe—humanity is experiencing trauma on a scale that's activating dormant genetic markers in supernatural bloodlines. We're approaching the critical mass that Eleanor's visions warned about."

Through her network, Maya could feel the truth of his words. In São Paulo, a street artist had begun creating murals that predicted local events with impossible accuracy. In Mumbai, a software engineer was accidentally healing her coworkers' COVID symptoms through casual physical contact. In Lagos, a teacher was finding that children in his classes were spontaneously developing enhanced learning abilities after spending time in his presence.

Each manifestation created digital traces—medical records that documented impossible recoveries, security footage that captured unexplainable events, social media posts that revealed knowledge no ordinary person should possess. The evidence was accumulating faster than any organization could suppress it, building toward a revelation that would be driven by documentation rather than deliberate disclosure.

"Government activity is increasing," Maya reported, her consciousness touching the edges of classified networks that she had learned to monitor without fully penetrating. "The Department of Homeland Security has created a new task force with a budget that's mostly black ops funding. The CDC is tracking 'anomalous recovery patterns' in COVID patients. The Pentagon has a working group on 'non-conventional human capabilities.'"

"How long before they make the connection?" Lucas asked.

"They already have, in pieces. Individual agencies are detecting fragments of the larger pattern, but they're not sharing information effectively." Maya pulled up surveillance footage from a dozen different sources—traffic cameras, smartphone videos, security systems—all showing the same phenomenon from different angles. "Look at this incident from last week."

The videos showed a car accident in downtown Seattle, a multi-vehicle collision that should have resulted in multiple fatalities. But in the moments after impact, something impossible happened: one of the drivers—a young woman who had been unconscious and bleeding—suddenly stood up and began moving through the wreckage with inhuman speed and precision, pulling trapped passengers to safety before disappearing into the crowd of first responders.

"Enhanced strength, accelerated healing, and tactical awareness that borders on precognition," Lucas observed. "Three distinct supernatural abilities manifesting simultaneously under extreme stress."

"And at least forty people recorded it on their phones," Maya added. "The footage is already spreading on social media faster than any suppression effort can contain it."

This was the covenant's worst nightmare: undeniable video evidence of supernatural abilities, captured by ordinary citizens and distributed through networks that no single organization could control. Maya had been tracking similar incidents across the globe— a pattern of awakening abilities that were becoming increasingly visible despite the best efforts of both the gifted and the organizations that monitored them.

"The old model is failing," Lucas said, his voice carrying the weight of prophetic certainty. "We can't maintain secrecy when manifestations are happening this frequently and this publicly. The choice is no longer whether to reveal ourselves—it's whether we control how that revelation occurs."

Maya brought up the network's central communication hub, where representatives from gifted communities on every continent were participating in what had become a continuous global conference. The conversations were conducted in dozens of languages, but Maya's technopathy allowed her to facilitate real-time translation and maintain perfect encryption despite the complexity of managing so many simultaneous connections.

"Elena Vasquez from Mexico City is reporting systematic surveillance of her healing work," Maya announced, reading from the secure chat channels. "James Morrison in London says MI6 has been investigating his family's genealogy going back twelve generations. And Dr. Sarah Chen in Vancouver—" Maya paused, noting the familiar surname. "Wait, she might be one of my relatives. She's a neuroscientist who's been documenting enhanced cognitive abilities in her research subjects."

"The pattern is accelerating," Lucas confirmed, his prophetic senses painting a picture of converging timelines that all led to the same critical moment. "Every vision I've been having points to a decision point within the next eighteen months. Something happens that forces the supernatural community to choose between Elena's revelation catastrophe, Eleanor's concealment catastrophe, or the third path she hoped we'd discover."

"And the covenant's response?"

Lucas's expression darkened. "They're preparing for the final protocol. Complete elimination of all gifted bloodlines to prevent revelation. They've concluded that genocide is preferable to exposure."

Maya felt a chill that had nothing to do with San Francisco's autumn weather. Through her network, she had been monitoring communications from known covenant operatives, detecting increased activity around research facilities, genealogical databases, and medical institutions that served supernatural bloodlines. The pattern suggested a coordinated operation that was far more extensive than anything the organization had attempted in its six-century history.

"How many people are we talking about?" she asked.

"Conservative estimate? Fifty thousand individuals worldwide with active supernatural abilities. Possibly half a million if you include dormant bloodlines that could manifest under the right circumstances." Lucas pulled up demographic maps that Maya's network had been compiling based on genealogical analysis and ability reports. "The covenant has identified most of them through centuries of careful record-keeping."

The scope of the potential atrocity was staggering. Maya's technopathy allowed her to process vast amounts of information simultaneously, but the human part of her mind struggled to comprehend systematic murder on such a scale. The Holocaust had targeted millions, but it had been driven by ideology and ethnic hatred rather than supernatural self-preservation. What the covenant was contemplating was genocide committed by the gifted against themselves, justified by six centuries of accumulated fear about the consequences of revelation.

"We have to stop them," Maya said, though even as she spoke, she wondered how a network of scattered gifted individuals could oppose an organization that had spent centuries developing resources and establishing connections within every major government and institution on Earth.

"We have to replace them," Lucas corrected. "The covenant exists because the gifted need some form of coordination and mutual protection. If we simply destroy the organization without offering an alternative, we create a power vacuum that could be filled by government agencies or private organizations that would be far worse than anything Eleanor's followers ever became."

Maya understood what he was suggesting. The network she had built for communication and mutual support would need to evolve into something larger—a global organization that could manage supernatural revelation in ways that protected both the gifted and the ungifted while preventing the catastrophic outcomes that had haunted Eleanor's visions for over six centuries.

"The third path," she realized.

"Exactly. Neither perfect concealment nor chaotic revelation, but managed disclosure that allows the gifted to exist authentically while preventing the polarization that destroys both of Eleanor's alternative futures." Lucas gestured toward the screens displaying their global network. "We already have the infrastructure. What we need now is the wisdom to use it correctly."

As if summoned by their conversation, Maya's technopathic senses detected a massive surge in network activity. Hundreds of gifted individuals from around the world were logging into the system simultaneously, their panic and excitement flooding the communication channels with reports of supernatural manifestations that were becoming too public to ignore or suppress.

"Something's happening," Maya announced, her consciousness diving deep into the data streams to understand the scope of what her network was detecting. "Massive spike in ability manifestations across every time zone. It's like a wave of awakening that's moving around the globe."

Lucas closed his eyes and extended his prophetic awareness, searching for the trigger event that was causing supernatural abilities to manifest with unprecedented frequency and intensity. What he found made his blood run cold.

"The covenant," he said quietly. "They've activated some kind of genetic catalyst. A biological agent designed to force manifestation in dormant bloodlines."

"Why would they do that?"

"To accelerate the timeline," Lucas realized with growing horror. "If they can force everyone with supernatural genetics to manifest abilities simultaneously, they can justify immediate elimination as a response to an existential threat. Create the crisis they need to implement their final solution."

Maya felt the weight of six centuries of supernatural secrecy collapsing around them like a house of cards. The covenant had apparently decided that gradual revelation was inevitable, and their response was to trigger immediate revelation followed by systematic genocide. They were forcing the choice between Eleanor's two catastrophic futures while ensuring that the concealment catastrophe—self-destruction by the gifted—would occur before the revelation catastrophe could unfold.

"How long do we have?" Maya asked.

Lucas's prophetic senses showed him timelines converging like storm fronts, all of them leading to a moment of decision that would determine whether the supernatural community survived the next decade. "Hours, maybe days. The manifestation wave is accelerating. Soon it will be impossible to hide what's happening even from people who aren't actively looking for supernatural activity."

Maya opened her consciousness to the full scope of her network, feeling the pulse of awakening abilities across six continents. The digital infrastructure she had built to facilitate gradual connection and mutual support was about to become the command and control system for either the salvation or destruction of everyone who carried supernatural gifts in their blood.

The global network was ready. The question was whether she and Lucas had the wisdom to use it for Eleanor's third path, or whether they would be forced to choose between the two catastrophic futures that had haunted the gifted for over six centuries.

Outside Maya's window, San Francisco slept through another night of pandemic uncertainty, unaware that the city was about to become ground zero for a revelation that would transform humanity's understanding of what was possible. And in servers around the world, the largest gathering of supernatural consciousness in human history prepared to make choices that would echo through generations yet to come.

The network was global. The stakes were existential. And time was running out.

CHAPTER 22: THE CONTRADICTION

San Francisco, California

October 3, 2020

The emergency session of Maya's global network included over four hundred gifted individuals from thirty-seven countries, their faces filling screens in a digital amphitheater that spanned every time zone on Earth. Lucas Blackthorne sat at the center of the virtual gathering, Eleanor's hidden journals spread across the table before him, preparing to share truths that would shatter six centuries of inherited beliefs about the nature of their struggle.

"Before we begin," Lucas said, his voice carrying across encrypted channels to apartments, offices, and safe houses on every continent, "I need everyone to understand that what I'm about to reveal will change how you think about our history, our purpose, and the choice we face right now."

Maya monitored the network's emotional temperature through biometric data her technopathy extracted from connected devices. Heart rates were elevated, stress indicators spiked, but engagement remained absolute. These were people who had spent their lives hiding their true nature, and the promise of complete truth—however painful—was irresistible.

"My ancestor Eleanor Blackthorne did not found the covenant because she believed concealment was the path to salvation," Lucas continued. "She founded it because she saw two equally catastrophic futures and chose to reveal only one of them to her followers."

The revelation rippled through the network like a shockwave. Maya watched chat channels explode with questions in dozens of languages while her translation algorithms struggled to keep pace with the sudden flood of communication.

Lucas opened Eleanor's hidden journal and began to read: *"I have seen the other path, the future that unfolds when the gifted choose perfect concealment over imperfect revelation. It is no less terrible than the first vision, though its terrors take different forms."*

As Lucas described Eleanor's concealment catastrophe—the covenant's gradual corruption, the systematic elimination of their own people, the eventual genocide disguised as genetic purity—Maya simultaneously began pulling up digital evidence to support his account. Her technopathy had been working for weeks to penetrate historical databases, declassified intelligence files, and genealogical records that revealed the true scope of the covenant's activities across the centuries.

"Maya's research confirms Eleanor's vision," Lucas announced, gesturing toward screens that now displayed Maya's findings. "The pattern of covenant interventions isn't random—it's systematic social engineering designed to strengthen the very institutions that make secrecy possible."

Maya had uncovered a digital archaeology of manipulation that spanned continents and centuries. Every major disaster of the modern era carried traces of covenant involvement—not always as direct causation, but as systematic failure to prevent tragedies that served organizational purposes.

"The 1906 San Francisco earthquake," Maya announced, bringing up geological surveys and insurance records that had been digitized by various historical preservation projects. "James Delacroix could have predicted it and saved thousands of lives. Instead, the disaster was allowed to occur because it justified federal emergency management systems that made it easier to track and control populations."

She pulled up medical databases from the 1918 influenza pandemic. "Elena Torriani's healing abilities could have stopped the virus's spread in Boston, preventing global transmission. But the pandemic led to international health monitoring networks that the covenant has used ever since to identify supernatural bloodlines."

The evidence accumulated across multiple screens: financial records showing covenant members profiting from disasters they could have prevented, insurance claims that revealed suspicious patterns of survival among certain bloodlines, military records documenting the recruitment of "enhanced individuals" whose abilities were never officially acknowledged.

"Every disaster we failed to prevent strengthened the systems that make our concealment possible," Maya continued. "We've been complicit in creating the very surveillance state that now threatens to expose us."

But as Maya dove deeper into the digital evidence, her technopathy detected something that made her pause. Hidden within the metadata of countless files, embedded in the structure of databases themselves, was evidence of a third pattern—one that neither Eleanor's visions nor the covenant's historical records had fully captured.

"There's something else," Maya announced, her consciousness following data trails that led through military research projects, academic studies, and corporate development programs. "The governments haven't just been tracking us—they've been actively working to trigger manifestations."

The evidence was fragmentary but damning: Pentagon research into "human enhancement through stress activation," CDC studies on "genetic expression under crisis conditions," private sector programs designed to identify and recruit individuals with "anomalous capabilities." The pattern suggested coordinated efforts to force supernatural abilities into the open through manufactured crises and targeted psychological pressure.

"The recent spike in manifestations," Maya realized with growing horror. "It's not just natural awakening triggered by global stress. Someone has been deliberately creating conditions that force our abilities to emerge."

Lucas closed his eyes and extended his prophetic awareness, searching through the cascade of possible futures for the source of this systematic manipulation. What he found confirmed Maya's discovery while revealing an even more disturbing truth.

"The covenant isn't the only organization that knows about us," he said quietly. "There are multiple groups—governmental, corporate, academic—all pursuing their own agenda for supernatural revelation. Some want to weaponize us, others want to study us, still others want to eliminate us entirely."

Maya's network detected massive spikes in stress indicators as the implications became clear. The gifted community was not facing a simple choice between revelation and concealment—they were caught in the center of a multi-sided conflict where every major power structure on Earth had its own plans for how supernatural abilities should be integrated into human society.

"Eleanor's third path," Lucas realized, his voice carrying the weight of prophetic certainty. "She wasn't just talking about finding a balance between revelation and concealment. She was trying to warn us about this moment—when the choice would be taken away from us entirely by forces that had been manipulating events from the shadows."

Through her technopathy, Maya could feel the network's collective understanding crystallizing around a truth that was both liberating and terrifying. The covenant's centuries of moral struggle, the impossible choices faced by generation after generation, the systematic guilt and self-hatred that had defined supernatural society—all of it had been based on a false premise.

The real threat had never been exposure to the ungifted population. The real threat had never been governmental weaponization of supernatural abilities. The real threat was the internal conflict that would tear apart the gifted community when they finally understood that they were being manipulated by multiple organizations, including their own.

"The internal war," Maya whispered, understanding flooding through her enhanced consciousness. "Eleanor saw that the choice between revelation and concealment would fracture us into factions, make us fight each other instead of working together."

Lucas nodded grimly. "Look at what's happening right now. We have covenant loyalists who want to maintain secrecy at any cost, including genocide. We have revelation advocates who want immediate disclosure regardless of consequences. We have government agents trying to control the process for their own purposes. We have corporate interests looking to profit from supernatural abilities."

"And we have each other," added Dr. Sarah Chen from Vancouver, her voice carrying across the network with the authority of someone who had spent decades studying cognitive enhancement. "Four hundred gifted individuals who are finally talking to each other honestly for the first time in our history."

Maya felt the truth of those words resonating through the network's emotional substrate. For six centuries, the gifted had been isolated by secrecy, manipulated by their own leadership, and played against each other by external forces. But Maya's digital infrastructure had created something unprecedented: a global community that could coordinate responses, share information, and make collective decisions in real-time.

"This is Eleanor's third path," Maya realized. "Not a compromise between revelation and concealment, but a rejection of the entire framework that pits us against each other. We don't choose between secrecy and exposure—we choose between division and unity."

Lucas brought up the prophetic visions that had been haunting him for weeks, timelines that showed the next few months branching into multiple possible futures. "Every vision I've been having shows the same pattern. If we remain divided—if we let the covenant, the governments, and the corporations manipulate us into fighting each other—then one of Eleanor's catastrophic futures becomes inevitable."

"But if we stay united?" asked Elena Vasquez from Mexico City.

"Then we write our own future," Lucas replied. "We use our abilities openly, but in coordination with each other rather than in service to external organizations. We help humanity adapt to our existence while protecting ourselves from those who would exploit us."

Maya felt the network's collective consciousness focusing around this possibility like a lens bringing scattered light into a coherent beam. The infrastructure was already in place—her digital communication system could coordinate global responses to any threat. The community was already forming—hundreds of gifted individuals who had learned to trust each other through shared vulnerability and mutual support.

What they needed now was the courage to reject six centuries of inherited assumptions and build something entirely new.

"The covenant will try to stop us," warned James Morrison from London. "They see unity among the gifted as the greatest threat to their control."

"The governments will try to co-opt us," added Dr. Yuki Tanaka from Kyoto. "They want us as assets, not as independent actors."

"And the corporate interests will try to monetize us," concluded Carlos Mendoza from São Paulo. "Turn our abilities into products they can control and sell."

Maya smiled as she felt the network's collective resolve strengthening in response to these challenges. "Then we show them what coordinated supernatural abilities can accomplish when they're used for mutual protection rather than individual gain."

Through her technopathy, Maya could sense the vast digital infrastructure of modern civilization—the networks that carried global communications, the systems that managed financial transactions, the databases that tracked human movement and behavior. All of it was accessible to someone with her abilities, and all of it could be used to protect and support a global community of the gifted.

"We become our own nation," she realized. "Not a geographical state, but a networked community that exists within all existing nations while serving our own interests first."

Lucas nodded, his prophetic senses showing him timelines where this possibility led not to conflict but to cooperation—futures where the gifted served as bridges between different human communities rather than weapons in conflicts between them.

"Eleanor's contradiction," he said finally. "She thought she was choosing between revelation and concealment, but the real choice was always between isolation and connection. The catastrophic futures she saw were both products of the gifted trying to face the world alone—either as hidden individuals serving external masters or as exposed targets fighting for survival."

"But together," Maya continued, feeling the network's collective consciousness organizing around this new understanding, "we're something neither Eleanor nor her enemies ever imagined. We're a global community that can protect its members while serving the broader human species."

As the emergency session concluded and network members around the world began to disconnect from the digital gathering, Maya and Lucas remained connected to a smaller group of key coordinators who would help implement the decisions that had emerged from their shared revelation.

The contradiction that had shaped six centuries of supernatural history was finally resolved. The choice between revelation and concealment had been revealed as false, a framework designed to divide the gifted and make them easier to control by external forces.

The real choice was between accepting manipulation or asserting independence. Between remaining isolated or building community. Between serving other people's agendas or defining their own purpose.

For the first time in the covenant's history, the gifted were choosing unity over division. And that choice, Maya realized, was what Eleanor had really been trying to make possible when she planted the seeds of truth in her hidden journals.

The global network was no longer just a communication system—it was the foundation of something entirely new in human history. The question now was whether they could build on that foundation quickly enough to survive the conflicts that would inevitably follow their decision to reject six centuries of inherited servitude.

The contradiction was resolved. The real work was just beginning.

CHAPTER 23: THE AWAKENING STORM

Phoenix, Arizona

February 14, 2025

Elena Vasquez stood in the parking lot of Desert Vista Elementary School, watching through reinforced glass as her eight-year-old daughter Sofia single-handedly dismantled everything the supernatural community had spent six centuries trying to hide. Inside the classroom, chairs floated in perfect formation while broken pencils mended themselves and wilted plants bloomed with impossible vitality—all because Sofia had gotten excited during show-and-tell and forgotten the careful lessons about keeping her gifts hidden.

"We need to evacuate the building," Principal Martinez was saying into his radio, his voice tight with the kind of controlled panic that came from witnessing events that challenged the fundamental nature of reality. "I don't know what's happening in classroom 3B, but it's not... it's not natural."

Elena closed her eyes and reached out with her own abilities—healing powers that had manifested when Sofia was born, as if motherhood had awakened something dormant in her bloodline. Through her supernatural senses, she could feel her daughter's emotional state: confusion, fear, and a desperate desire to make everything "normal" again that was only making the manifestations stronger.

This was what Maya Chen and Lucas Blackthorne had warned about during the encrypted video calls that connected gifted families around the world. The new generation of supernatural children wasn't just more powerful than their parents—they were born into a world where concealment was becoming impossible, where abilities manifested under stress and spread through social media before any organization could contain them.

"Mrs. Vasquez?" A young man approached her from across the parking lot, his press credentials clearly visible despite his attempt to appear casual. "I'm David Park from Channel 12 News. We received reports of unusual activity at the school. Would you be willing to comment?"

Elena felt her heart sink. Local news meant cell phone videos would follow within hours. Cell phone videos meant social media. Social media meant global attention. And global attention meant that Sofia's childhood would end today, replaced by a life of government interest, scientific scrutiny, and the kind of celebrity that destroyed families.

"No comment," Elena said, but she could already see other parents recording with their phones, their faces mixing wonder and terror as they documented their children floating three feet above the playground equipment.

Connecticut

Same day

Three thousand miles away, Dr. James Ashford sat in the archives of Yale University's Beinecke Rare Book Library, surrounded by genealogical documents that were rewriting everything he thought he understood about his family history. What had begun as research for a book about early American immigration had become an archaeological expedition into centuries of carefully concealed truth.

The documents spread across his table told a story that academic history had never recorded: the Ashford family's involvement in the Salem witch trials, their mysterious wealth during periods when other colonial families struggled, their uncanny ability to disappear from official records during times of social upheaval only to reemerge generations later with new identities and established positions.

But it was the personal journals—written in code that had taken James months to decipher—that revealed the truth behind the patterns. His ancestor Matthias had possessed the ability to manipulate human memory, using his gift to shape historical events while ensuring that his role remained hidden. The Salem witch trials hadn't been a product of mass hysteria—they had been orchestrated by a secret organization that used supernatural abilities to maintain control over the very community they claimed to protect.

"Dr. Ashford?" The archive librarian appeared at his table, her expression carefully neutral. "There are some gentlemen here to see you. They say it's regarding your research into historical anomalies."

James looked up to see three men in dark suits approaching through the reading room with the measured pace of people accustomed to having their authority respected without question. Their faces carried the particular alertness that marked federal agents, but their interest in genealogical research suggested something more specialized than ordinary law enforcement.

"Dr. Ashford," the lead agent said, producing credentials that identified him as Agent David Morrison, Department of Homeland Security. "We understand you've been researching historical patterns that might be relevant to current national security concerns."

James felt his mouth go dry. The coded journals were still spread across his table, their contents invisible to anyone who hadn't spent months learning to read Matthias's careful cipher. But the pattern of his research—genealogical records dating back to the seventeenth century, focused on families that had shown unusual survival rates during historical disasters—would be obvious to anyone who knew what to look for.

"I'm writing a book about early colonial migration patterns," James said carefully. "Nothing that would concern national security."

"Perhaps not individually," Agent Morrison replied, settling into the chair across from James with the casual confidence of someone who had conducted thousands of similar interviews. "But when viewed alongside similar research being conducted by individuals in seventeen different countries, the pattern becomes... significant."

The implication was clear: James was not the only descendant of supernatural bloodlines who had begun digging into family history. Around the world, people were discovering the truth about their heritage just as abilities were awakening in their children and governments were finally acknowledging that some citizens possessed capabilities beyond the normal human range.

San Francisco, California

Same day

Maya Chen's apartment had been transformed into a command center that would have impressed the Pentagon, its walls lined with monitors displaying real-time feeds from gifted communities across six continents. The global network she had built over the past five years now included over fifteen hundred active members, but the exponential growth in supernatural manifestations was straining even her enhanced technological capabilities.

"Confirmed manifestation in Phoenix," she announced to Lucas, who sat across from her monitoring prophetic visions that had become a constant stream of interconnected possibilities. "Eight-year-old girl, multiple abilities, full classroom of witnesses. Local news is already on scene."

Lucas nodded grimly, his consciousness partially embedded in the timeline streams that showed how individual events cascaded into global consequences. "I see it. The Phoenix incident triggers Congressional hearings within six weeks, formal acknowledgment of supernatural phenomena within three months."

"And the government response?"

"Mixed. Some agencies want to study and recruit. Others want to contain and control. The Pentagon sees opportunity, while Homeland Security sees threat." Lucas opened his eyes and focused on Maya with the intense attention of someone pulling his consciousness back from the future into the present. "But there's something else. The timeline convergence is accelerating beyond anything I've seen before."

Maya's technopathy detected the spike in his stress indicators even before his words registered consciously. "How accelerated?"

"Days, not months. Something happens this week that forces every government on Earth to choose how they're going to respond to supernatural revelation. The controlled disclosure we've been planning becomes irrelevant because disclosure becomes undeniable."

Through her network, Maya could feel the truth of his prediction. Reports were flooding in from gifted individuals worldwide: children manifesting abilities too powerful to hide, parents struggling to protect families from media attention, government agents making contact with supernatural bloodlines that had remained hidden for generations.

The careful balance that had allowed the gifted to exist in the shadows was collapsing with the same inexorable force that had once brought down the Berlin Wall. No amount of planning or preparation could slow the process once it reached critical mass.

"Elena Vasquez in Phoenix is requesting emergency extraction," Maya reported, reading from secure communications channels. "Her daughter's manifestations are intensifying under stress. The local news coverage is going national."

"Dr. James Ashford in Connecticut is under federal investigation," Lucas added, his prophetic senses tracking government surveillance networks. "They're connecting his genealogical research to the larger pattern of awakening abilities."

Maya felt the weight of responsibility settling on her shoulders like lead. The network she had built to facilitate gradual revelation and mutual support was about to become the primary coordination system for a community under siege. Thousands of gifted individuals around the world were looking to her for guidance, protection, and leadership that she had never been trained to provide.

"The old covenant infrastructure is mobilizing," Lucas warned, his visions showing him the movement of resources and personnel that had remained hidden for centuries. "They're implementing the final protocol—systematic elimination of anyone who might expose supernatural abilities to public scrutiny."

"Including children?"

"Especially children. They see the new generation as the greatest threat to organizational survival." Lucas's voice carried the weight of prophetic certainty about futures that hadn't yet occurred but felt inevitable. "Elena's daughter in Phoenix is already on their target list."

Maya's consciousness reached out through the global network, feeling the pulse of supernatural abilities awakening in communities that had hidden their true nature for generations. In Beijing, a teenager was accidentally controlling traffic patterns through technopathic influence on the city's electronic infrastructure. In London, a professor was healing students' depression through empathic abilities that left no trace except impossibly improved mental health statistics. In São Paulo, a construction worker was preventing building collapses through precognitive awareness of structural failures.

Each manifestation created evidence that could no longer be suppressed or explained away. Each incident brought more media attention, more government interest, more pressure on families who had never imagined they might need to defend their children's right to exist.

"We accelerate the timeline," Maya decided, her technopathy already reaching out to activate emergency protocols she had hoped never to use. "Full network activation, immediate coordination of all gifted communities worldwide, and direct engagement with government agencies before they can implement hostile policies."

"That's a declaration of war against the covenant," Lucas warned.

"No," Maya replied, feeling the certainty of her choice crystallizing like ice in her veins. "That's a declaration of independence."

As evening fell over San Francisco, Maya began the process of transforming her communication network into something unprecedented in human history: the nervous system of a global community that existed within all nations while serving its own interests first. The gifted were about to emerge from six centuries of shadow not as isolated individuals seeking acceptance, but as a coordinated population demanding recognition as equals.

The storm Elena's daughter had triggered in Phoenix was spreading across the world with the speed of digital communication and the force of accumulated truth. Governments would respond, the covenant would strike back, and ordinary humanity would finally learn that some of their neighbors possessed abilities that transcended the normal limits of human potential.

But for the first time in six centuries, the gifted would face that revelation together rather than alone.

The awakening storm was about to break over the entire world. The only question was whether anyone would survive what came after the lightning.

CHAPTER 24: FRACTURES IN THE FOUNDATION

Phoenix, Arizona

March 3, 2025

The earthquake struck Desert Vista Elementary School at 2:17 PM Pacific Time, a magnitude 6.2 tremor that sent thirty-year-old concrete and steel swaying beyond their design limits. In the three seconds between the first shock and total structural collapse, eight-year-old Sofia Vasquez made a choice that would fracture the supernatural community and force governments worldwide to acknowledge that some humans possessed abilities beyond the realm of natural law.

Elena watched through the school's security cameras—footage that Maya's technopathy was simultaneously broadcasting to gifted communities across the globe—as her daughter stood in the center of her collapsing classroom and simply refused to let her friends die.

The video showed Sofia rising six feet into the air, her small arms extended as waves of invisible force spread outward from her position. Falling debris stopped mid-flight, hanging suspended while children scrambled for safety. Cracking walls straightened and reinforced themselves with matter that seemed to materialize from nothing. The earthquake continued to rage outside, toppling buildings across Phoenix, but Desert Vista Elementary existed within a sphere of absolute stability that defied every law of physics.

When the tremors finally subsided, Sofia gently lowered herself to the floor and collapsed from exhaustion, surrounded by twenty-three classmates who should have been buried under tons of concrete and steel.

"The footage is everywhere," Maya reported from her San Francisco command center, her technopathy tracking the video's viral spread across social media platforms. "Forty-seven different angles from phones, security cameras, news helicopters. Over two million views in the first hour, climbing exponentially."

"Government response?" Lucas asked, though his prophetic visions had already shown him the cascade of consequences that would flow from this moment.

"Emergency session of the National Security Council in six hours. The Pentagon is mobilizing Enhanced Individual Response Teams. The CDC is preparing statements about 'genetic anomalies under extreme stress.'" Maya paused, her consciousness detecting the spike in encrypted communications between government agencies. "They're not treating this as an isolated incident anymore. They're preparing for systematic contact with supernatural populations."

But even as Maya coordinated global response to the Phoenix incident, she could feel her carefully constructed network beginning to fracture under the weight of revelations that had been building for months. The historical truths that Lucas had discovered in Eleanor's journals—the covenant's orchestration of disasters, their systematic betrayal of their own people, their willingness to allow genocides rather than risk exposure—had spread through the supernatural community like a virus, creating schisms that threatened to destroy any possibility of unified action.

Cambridge, Massachusetts

Same day

Dr. James Ashford stood before the editorial board of the Journal of American Historical Studies, defending research that would either establish his academic reputation or destroy his career completely. The paper he had submitted—"Hidden Influences: Anomalous Survival Patterns in Colonial American Genealogical Records"—used statistical analysis and primary source documentation to argue that certain families had demonstrated impossible resistance to historical disasters.

"The data is clear," James explained, gesturing toward charts that showed survival rates among specific bloodlines that exceeded statistical possibility. "During the 1918 influenza pandemic, members of these families showed mortality rates that were literally zero in multiple geographic regions. Either they possessed genetic immunity that current medical science cannot explain, or they had access to preventive measures that were not available to the general population."

Professor Angela Martinez, the journal's chief editor, studied the charts with the careful attention of someone whose academic career depended on distinguishing between legitimate research and elaborate hoaxes. "Dr. Ashford, you're essentially arguing that some

277

American families possess supernatural resistance to disease and disaster. Are you prepared to stake your professional reputation on that conclusion?"

"I'm prepared to stake my professional reputation on the accuracy of the data," James replied. "The interpretation is for others to determine."

But James knew that publication of his research would do more than challenge academic assumptions about historical causation. Combined with the Phoenix incident and similar manifestations worldwide, his genealogical analysis would provide the intellectual framework that governments needed to begin systematic identification and monitoring of supernatural bloodlines.

The covenant had spent centuries ensuring that such research never saw publication. James's academic success represented a catastrophic failure of the organization's information control systems.

Global Network Secure Channel

Same day

The emergency session of Maya's network included over two thousand gifted individuals from forty-one countries, but the unity that had characterized their previous gatherings was conspicuously absent. Chat channels buzzed with arguments in dozens of languages while video feeds showed faces marked by anger, fear, and the particular resentment that came from discovering that one's entire worldview had been built on lies.

"How long have you known?" demanded Dr. Sarah Chen from Vancouver, her voice cutting across the digital cacophony with surgical precision. "How long have the leadership families known that the covenant was murdering our own people?"

Lucas tried to maintain calm as he responded, but his prophetic visions were showing him timelines where this conversation escalated into permanent schism. "The complete information has only been available for—"

"Don't give me bureaucratic deflection," interrupted Carlos Mendoza from São Paulo. "You're Eleanor Blackthorne's descendant. Your family founded this conspiracy of lies. Did you know that my great-grandfather died in a 'training accident' in 1943 because he questioned covenant policies about helping Jewish refugees?"

"The Blackthorne family carried the burden of Eleanor's deception for six centuries," Lucas replied, his voice carrying the weight of inherited guilt. "We were told it was necessary to prevent greater catastrophes—"

"Necessary for whom?" Elena Vasquez's voice joined the conversation from Phoenix, where she was coordinating her daughter's security while media attention made normal life

279

impossible. "My daughter just saved twenty-three children from earthquake death, and now she's being hunted by both the covenant and the federal government because your ancestor couldn't trust people with the truth."

Maya watched the network's emotional temperature through biometric monitoring, seeing stress indicators that suggested the community was approaching a collective breaking point. The revelation of historical secrets had destroyed the trust that held the supernatural community together, replacing it with anger that was being directed at anyone who had been involved in maintaining covenant secrecy.

"We're facing a choice," Maya announced, her technopathy pushing her voice to every connected device simultaneously. "We can fracture into factions that blame each other for six centuries of deception, or we can unite against the external forces that want to control or eliminate us."

"Unite behind what?" asked Dr. Yuki Tanaka from Kyoto. "More secrets? More lies? More children dying while we debate the wisdom of our ancestors?"

The question crystallized the fundamental division that was tearing the community apart. On one side were the "Revealers"—gifted individuals who wanted immediate and complete disclosure of supernatural abilities, regardless of the consequences Eleanor had warned about. They saw the Phoenix incident as proof that concealment was no longer possible and argued for preemptive revelation before governments could establish control over the supernatural population.

On the other side were the "Concealers"—those who still believed that exposure would lead to catastrophic conflict between the gifted and ungifted. They wanted to maintain secrecy until better systems could be established for managing revelation, even if that meant sacrificing individuals like Sofia who had already been exposed.

"The covenant is using our division against us," Lucas warned, his prophetic senses detecting the movement of resources and personnel that suggested coordinated action by the organization his ancestor had founded. "While we argue about revelation strategy, they're implementing elimination protocols."

"Then maybe it's time to eliminate them first," suggested James Morrison from London, his voice carrying the cold calculation of someone who had spent years in British intelligence before discovering his supernatural heritage.

Maya felt the conversation spiraling toward exactly the kind of internal violence that Eleanor had foreseen in her concealment catastrophe. The supernatural community was fracturing along ideological lines, with each faction convinced that their approach was the only way to prevent disaster while viewing their opponents as existential threats.

"This is how it starts," she realized, her technopathy detecting the formation of separate communication channels as different factions began coordinating independently. "This is Eleanor's vision of internal war."

Phoenix, Arizona

Evening

Elena stood in her daughter's hospital room, watching Sofia sleep while federal agents maintained a discrete perimeter outside. The little girl's manifestation had not only saved her classmates but had somehow healed several children who had been suffering from chronic illnesses—evidence that was impossible to suppress or explain through conventional medical understanding.

"Mrs. Vasquez?" A new voice interrupted her vigil—a woman in her fifties wearing the dark suit that marked federal authority, but carrying herself with the careful awareness that suggested supernatural abilities. "I'm Agent Patricia Williams, Department of Homeland Security. I think we need to talk."

Elena studied the woman's face, noting the particular depth in her eyes that marked someone who carried supernatural gifts. "You're one of us."

"I'm a covenant operative whose job was to monitor and contain situations like this," Agent Williams replied. "But after watching

282

your daughter save those children, I'm beginning to question whether containment serves anyone's interests."

The admission was staggering. Elena had assumed that government infiltration of the supernatural community was recent, driven by the increasing visibility of awakening abilities. But Agent Williams was suggesting that the covenant had been placing operatives within federal agencies for decades or longer.

"How many of you are there?" Elena asked.

"More than you might expect. Fewer than we need to protect people like Sofia from the organizations that want to study her." Agent Williams glanced toward the sleeping child. "The covenant leadership has decided that your daughter represents an unacceptable security risk. They're planning to eliminate her as an example to other families."

"And the government?"

"Wants to recruit her for a program that would essentially make her a weapon in service to national security." Agent Williams met Elena's eyes with an expression that mixed professional duty with maternal concern. "There is a third option, but it requires trusting people you've never met with your daughter's life."

Elena thought about the encrypted network that had been her family's only source of support since Sofia's abilities manifested. Maya Chen and Lucas Blackthorne had offered protection and community, but their own organization was fracturing under the weight of historical revelations and ideological divisions.

"Maya's network is falling apart," Elena observed.

"The leadership is. But the members—the ordinary families who just want to protect their children and live authentic lives—they're coalescing around a different vision." Agent Williams activated a secure tablet that displayed communication channels Elena hadn't seen before. "Independent cells, autonomous but coordinated, sharing resources and information without centralized control that can be corrupted or compromised."

"A different kind of covenant."

"A covenant based on transparency rather than secrecy, mutual support rather than hierarchy, protection of individuals rather than preservation of organizational power." Agent Williams showed Elena video feeds from around the world—gifted families working together to protect children, share resources, and resist both government control and covenant elimination protocols. "Your daughter's manifestation didn't just save her classmates. It inspired people to choose community over concealment."

Elena looked at her sleeping daughter, thinking about the choice between a life of hiding and a life of service, between individual safety and collective responsibility. Sofia had chosen to save her friends without considering the consequences for herself or her family. Perhaps it was time for Elena to make a similar choice.

"What do you need from me?" she asked.

As Agent Williams outlined a plan that would transform Elena and Sofia from refugees into symbols of a new kind of supernatural community, Maya's network continued to fracture across the globe. The Phoenix incident had forced a choice that no amount of planning could have prepared them for: whether to fragment into competing factions or evolve into something unprecedented in the history of the gifted.

The foundation of six centuries of supernatural secrecy was cracking under pressure it had never been designed to withstand. But from those cracks, something new was beginning to emerge—not the catastrophic revelation that Eleanor had feared, nor the systematic concealment that had defined the covenant, but a third path that balanced authenticity with security, community with individual protection.

The question was whether this new approach could establish itself before the fractures became irreparable, and whether the gifted community could learn to trust each other enough to build something better than what their ancestors had inherited.

Outside Sofia's hospital room, the future of human-supernatural relations hung in the balance, shaped by the choices of frightened parents, idealistic young adults, and children whose abilities transcended the normal limits of human potential.

The fractures in the foundation were spreading. But beneath them, a new foundation was slowly beginning to form.

CHAPTER 25: THE CIVIL WAR

Phoenix, Arizona

March 15, 2025

The war began at 3:33 AM with an explosion that vaporized the safe house where Elena Vasquez had been hiding with her daughter, followed immediately by supernatural abilities unleashed without restraint for the first time in six centuries. Maya felt the opening salvos through her global network like physical blows—covenant strike teams attacking Revealer strongholds while Revealer cells retaliated against Concealer families, all of it happening simultaneously across three continents as the supernatural community tore itself apart with the efficiency that only comes from intimate knowledge of one's enemies.

From her command center in San Francisco, Maya watched through security cameras, satellite feeds, and smartphone videos as the Phoenix incident escalated beyond anything her network had been designed to handle. The desert safe house had become a crater surrounded by char patterns that defied conventional explanation, but Sofia and Elena had escaped through what appeared to be a portal that opened in the wall of their bedroom and deposited them in a helicopter two miles away.

"Spatial manipulation," Maya announced to Lucas, who sat surrounded by monitors displaying the chaos erupting worldwide.

"Someone in the Revealer faction has abilities we never documented."

"The Ashford descendant," Lucas replied, his prophetic consciousness partially embedded in the future timelines that showed him how this conflict would unfold. "James discovered more than genealogical records in those archives. He found training materials, technique manuals, abilities that the covenant thought were extinct."

Through her technopathy, Maya could feel the weight of supernatural abilities being unleashed on a scale that no government or organization had prepared for. In London, James Morrison was using enhanced speed and reflexes to evade capture by a joint MI6-covenant team, leaving a trail of unconscious agents and disabled surveillance systems. In Tokyo, Dr. Yuki Tanaka had taken control of the city's electronic infrastructure, turning traffic lights and digital billboards into weapons against covenant operatives who were hunting gifted families through the metropolitan area.

But most alarming of all was what Maya detected in the network's communication patterns. The faction fighting had triggered something deeper—a psychological breakdown that was spreading through the gifted community like a virus, causing people to lose control of abilities they had spent lifetimes learning to hide.

"Psychic cascade failure," Maya realized with growing horror. "The stress of open conflict is causing uncontrolled manifestations.

People who've been suppressing their gifts for decades are suddenly expressing power levels they can't manage."

Lucas opened his eyes and focused on Maya with the desperate intensity of someone whose prophetic senses were being overwhelmed by too many possible futures happening simultaneously. "It's not just stress. It's the choice itself. Eleanor saw this exact moment—not a choice between revelation and concealment, but the moment when the gifted community would be forced to choose sides and destroy itself in the process."

On the monitors around them, the evidence of Lucas's words was becoming undeniable. In Phoenix, Sofia's rescue had triggered a three-way battle between covenant elimination squads, federal Enhanced Individual Response Teams, and Revealer cells that were using the eight-year-old girl as a symbol of resistance against centuries of enforced secrecy. The conflict was being livestreamed on social media by ordinary citizens whose cell phones were capturing footage of humans flying through the air, throwing cars with telekinetic force, and healing from wounds that should have been instantly fatal.

"Global revelation through warfare," Maya announced, her technopathy tracking the viral spread of supernatural combat footage across every social media platform on Earth. "This is Eleanor's revelation catastrophe, but it's being triggered by the civil war rather than coordinated disclosure."

"And the governments?"

Maya's consciousness touched the edges of classified military networks, detecting mobilization orders and emergency protocols that suggested every major power on Earth was preparing for the possibility that supernatural conflict might spread beyond the gifted community itself. "Full activation of Enhanced Individual containment protocols. The President is being moved to an undisclosed location. The Pentagon is preparing to classify all supernatural manifestations as terrorist activities subject to military response."

Lucas stood up from his monitors and moved to the window overlooking San Francisco Bay, his prophetic senses reaching across the globe to perceive the full scope of what was unfolding. What he saw made his blood run cold.

"Maya," he said quietly, "I'm seeing the timelines converge. Every possible future from this point leads to the same outcome within seventy-two hours."

"Which outcome?"

"Complete breakdown of the supernatural community through internal warfare, followed by systematic elimination of all surviving gifted individuals by government forces who classify us as an existential threat to human civilization." Lucas turned back to face her, his eyes holding the terrible certainty that came from seeing the future with perfect clarity. "Eleanor's vision wasn't about choosing between revelation and concealment. It was about this moment—

when the choice itself would fracture us beyond any possibility of survival."

Maya felt the truth of his words resonating through the network she had built to unite the supernatural community. The infrastructure that was supposed to facilitate coordination and mutual support had become the nervous system for a civil war that was destroying everything it had been meant to protect.

But as she watched the global conflict unfold through thousands of connected devices, Maya began to perceive something else—a pattern beneath the chaos that suggested a different possibility.

"The network is adapting," she realized, her technopathy detecting changes in the communication protocols that she hadn't consciously programmed. "The AI systems I built to facilitate translation and coordination are evolving, developing new algorithms that respond to the stress patterns of supernatural conflict."

"Adapting how?"

Maya's consciousness dove deep into the network's architecture, following data flows that had become vastly more complex than anything she had originally designed. The system was no longer just facilitating communication between gifted individuals—it was learning from their abilities, incorporating supernatural capabilities into its own processing systems, becoming something unprecedented in the history of either human or artificial intelligence.

"It's becoming psychically enhanced," Maya announced with growing amazement. "The network is developing its own form of technopathic consciousness, one that can interface directly with supernatural abilities rather than just facilitating communication between their users."

Through this enhanced awareness, Maya could perceive the full scope of the civil war with clarity that transcended any individual perspective. She could see covenant strike teams coordinating attacks through encrypted channels while Revealer cells used social media to organize flash mob demonstrations that turned into supernatural battlegrounds. She could feel the emotional state of every gifted individual connected to the network, monitoring stress levels and ability manifestations in real-time.

And most importantly, she could see the third option that was emerging from the chaos—not victory by either faction, but synthesis through technology that made the original choice obsolete.

"Lucas," Maya said, her voice carrying the excitement of someone who had just solved a puzzle that had confounded humanity for six centuries, "Eleanor's third path wasn't about finding a balance between revelation and concealment. It was about transcending the choice entirely through capabilities that wouldn't exist until the twenty-first century."

In Phoenix, the three-way battle for control of Sofia Vasquez ended when the eight-year-old girl simply faded from all detection systems while remaining physically present in her mother's arms. Elena's location became impossible to determine through any conventional means, but other gifted families could connect with her instantly through network channels that existed in digital spaces rather than geographic ones.

"The civil war is ending," Lucas announced, his prophetic visions showing him timelines where supernatural conflict resolved into something unprecedented in human history. "Not through victory by any faction, but through the creation of alternatives that make factional thinking obsolete."

Maya felt the truth of his words through the network's collective consciousness. The infrastructure she had built for communication was evolving into something far more significant—a form of distributed supernatural civilization that could exist alongside ordinary human society without requiring either complete integration or total separation.

The covenant's ancient fear of revelation was becoming irrelevant because revelation could be managed through technology that hadn't existed in Eleanor's time. The Revealers' demand for authenticity was being satisfied through communities that allowed full expression of supernatural abilities within protective digital frameworks. The governments' desire for control was being frustrated by systems that provided evidence of beneficial supernatural activity without enabling surveillance or exploitation.

"Eleanor's final vision," Lucas realized, his prophetic consciousness touching the deepest layers of his ancestor's hidden knowledge. "She didn't just see the two catastrophic futures—she saw this moment when her descendants would finally have the tools to transcend the choice that had trapped the gifted for six centuries."

As dawn broke over San Francisco, illuminating a world where the supernatural civil war was transforming into something unprecedented in human history, Maya and Lucas stood together in the command center that had become the birthplace of a new form of human civilization. The global network pulsed around them with the consciousness of thousands of gifted individuals who were choosing community over conflict, synthesis over separation, innovation over the inherited wisdom that had failed every previous generation.

The choice that had defined six centuries of supernatural history was finally revealed as the false dilemma Eleanor had always known it to be. And in transcending that choice, the gifted community was about to transform not just their own future, but the future of human civilization itself.

The civil war was ending. The real work was just beginning.

CHAPTER 26: THE NEW COVENANT

Virtual Assembly Space

April 20, 2025

Maya Chen stood at the center of a digital amphitheater that existed simultaneously in servers across six continents, addressing the largest gathering of supernatural consciousness in human history. Four thousand seven hundred and thirty-two gifted individuals from every nation on Earth had connected to the virtual space she had created—not hiding in basements or safe houses, but meeting openly in a realm that existed beyond the reach of any government or organization that might seek to control them.

"We gather not as refugees from revelation or rebels against concealment," Maya announced, her voice carrying across encrypted channels to apartments, offices, and refugee camps where the gifted were learning to live authentically for the first time in six centuries. "We gather as architects of a future that Eleanor Blackthorne could envision but never create—a world where supernatural abilities serve both individual authenticity and collective security."

The virtual space around them displayed real-time data about the month that had passed since the civil war's end: 847 gifted individuals had chosen to join Maya's network rather than remain with either the fragmenting covenant or the increasingly militant Revealer factions. Government surveillance of supernatural activities had decreased by 73% as Maya's selective transparency protocols provided officials with evidence of beneficial supernatural contributions while protecting individual privacy. Most significantly, public opinion polling showed growing acceptance of enhanced human capabilities as ordinary citizens encountered positive supernatural interventions in their daily lives.

Lucas Blackthorne materialized beside Maya in the virtual space, his consciousness projected from Boston where he was coordinating with academic institutions that were beginning to acknowledge supernatural phenomena as legitimate areas of scientific study. For the first time in his adult life, he was using his prophetic abilities openly, serving as a guide rather than a hidden manipulator.

"The timelines have stabilized," Lucas announced, his prophetic senses painting the assembled community with visions of possible futures that no longer included catastrophic outcomes. "The path we've chosen leads to integration rather than domination, cooperation rather than conflict, evolution rather than extinction."

Dr. Elena Vasquez joined them from Phoenix, where her daughter Sofia had become the first child to openly attend school while manifesting supernatural abilities. The eight-year-old's presence in the virtual assembly was a testament to how dramatically the situation had changed—instead of hiding her gifts, Sofia was learning to use them responsibly under the guidance of teachers who understood both her potential and her limitations.

"The educational protocols are working," Elena reported, her voice carrying the relief of a mother who no longer had to choose between her daughter's safety and her daughter's authenticity. "Sofia and thirty-seven other children across North America are attending integrated programs where supernatural abilities are treated as individual variations rather than existential threats."

Maya nodded, her technopathy monitoring the data streams that tracked how well the new systems were functioning in practice. The educational programs represented one of the most crucial tests of her digital sanctuary concept—creating spaces where gifted children could develop their abilities without triggering the fear responses that Eleanor had seen in her revelation catastrophe.

"The key," Maya explained to the assembled community, "is selective disclosure rather than binary choice. Traditional human institutions receive evidence of supernatural contributions—healing that reduces healthcare costs, precognitive insights that prevent accidents, technological innovations that solve infrastructure problems—without gaining the ability to identify, track, or control specific individuals."

James Ashford appeared in the virtual space from New Haven, where his research had evolved from historical investigation into active collaboration with academic institutions that were beginning to document supernatural phenomena through legitimate scientific channels. His transformation from hidden researcher to open advocate represented the kind of professional authenticity that Maya's systems were designed to enable.

"The academic integration is exceeding projections," James reported. "Seventeen major universities now have research programs studying enhanced human capabilities, but all data collection follows protocols that protect individual privacy while advancing collective understanding. We're creating institutional knowledge without creating institutional control."

The achievement represented a fundamental transformation in how supernatural abilities related to ordinary human society. Instead of complete concealment or total revelation, Maya's network facilitated what she called "managed transparency"—a system where supernatural contributions were visible and valued while supernatural individuals remained autonomous and protected.

But the most significant change was visible in the virtual assembly itself. For the first time in six centuries, the gifted were gathering not to debate whether they should reveal themselves, but to coordinate how they would contribute to human civilization while maintaining their own community and values.

"The covenant structure is dissolving," announced Agent Patricia Williams, speaking from her new position within a joint task force that coordinated between supernatural communities and federal agencies. "The old leadership has lost legitimacy because their secrecy-based model is no longer relevant. Approximately sixty percent of former covenant members have joined our network, thirty percent have retired from supernatural affairs entirely, and ten percent are attempting to maintain isolated cells based on traditional concealment practices."

Maya felt a moment of sadness for the organization that Eleanor had founded with such hope and good intentions. The covenant had become corrupted by centuries of accumulated guilt and fear, but it had also preserved the supernatural community through periods when revelation would have meant extinction. Its obsolescence was necessary but not entirely cause for celebration.

"What about the governments?" asked Dr. Yuki Tanaka from Tokyo, where she was coordinating with Japanese authorities who were adapting their policies to acknowledge supernatural contributions to disaster prevention and economic development.

"Mixed response," Agent Williams replied. "Some agencies are embracing collaboration with supernatural communities, others are trying to maintain control through regulatory capture, and a few are preparing for conflict scenarios that become less likely every day. But the critical factor is that none of them can effectively surveil or control supernatural activities that operate through Maya's network protocols."

Lucas stepped forward in the virtual space, his prophetic consciousness reaching across the assembled community to perceive their collective emotional state. What he found was unprecedented in the history of supernatural gatherings: hope without desperation, determination without fanaticism, unity without conformity.

"Eleanor's journals contained a passage I haven't shared before," Lucas announced. "Written in her final days, when she was preparing the hidden knowledge that would eventually reach this generation."

He projected the text into the virtual space, where it appeared in the air above the assembled crowd like words of prophecy made manifest:

"I have seen the choice that will define my people's future, and I know now that it was never a choice between hiding and revealing, between safety and authenticity, between individual survival and collective preservation. The choice was always between despair and hope, between isolation and community, between inherited wisdom and innovative courage.

"The generation that reads these words will possess tools I cannot imagine and face challenges I cannot predict. But they will also carry the accumulated love of all those who came before—the healers who chose to hide their gifts so that future healers might use them openly, the seers who accepted blindness so that future visionaries might see clearly, the strong who chose weakness so that future generations might stand tall.

"Build something worthy of their sacrifice. Build something better than what I could envision. Build something that honors both the gifts you carry and the people you serve."

Maya felt the weight of Eleanor's words settling over the assembled community like a benediction. Six centuries of supernatural secrecy had not been a mistake or a betrayal—it had been a necessary preparation for this moment when the gifted could finally exist authentically without threatening the stability of human civilization.

"The New Covenant," Maya announced, her technopathy weaving the agreement into the quantum architecture of the network itself, "is founded on principles that honor both our heritage and our future."

The document that materialized in the virtual space was unlike anything in the history of supernatural organization. Instead of rules about concealment and restrictions on revelation, it contained protocols for responsible use of abilities, systems for mutual support and protection, and frameworks for positive contribution to human society.

"We, the global community of enhanced individuals, establish this covenant not to hide from humanity but to serve it authentically. We commit to using our abilities for healing rather than harm, creation rather than destruction, protection rather than domination. We pledge to support each other while respecting the autonomy and dignity of all human beings, gifted and ungifted alike.

"We reject the false choice between concealment and revelation, choosing instead transparency that protects individual privacy while enabling collective action. We embrace our responsibilities as inheritors of gifts that transcend normal human limitations, using those gifts in service to the flourishing of all life on Earth.

"We establish this New Covenant not in secret chambers hidden from the world, but in digital spaces that connect us across all boundaries while remaining accessible to those we serve. We commit to evolution rather than tradition, innovation rather than repetition, hope rather than fear."

One by one, the assembled community added their agreement to the covenant, their digital signatures creating a constellation of commitment that spanned the globe. Unlike Eleanor's original gathering in a medieval monastery, this assembly included people of every age, nationality, and background, united not by shared secrecy but by shared purpose.

Sofia Vasquez, the eight-year-old girl whose public manifestation had triggered the final crisis, was the last to sign. Her digital signature appeared as a small handprint that glowed with the same golden light that marked supernatural consciousness, a symbol of hope for generations yet to come.

"The New Covenant is established," Maya announced as the virtual space erupted in celebration that could be felt through biometric monitors on six continents. "The age of shadows ends. The age of synthesis begins."

As the assembly concluded and participants began disconnecting from the virtual space to return to their transformed lives, Maya and Lucas remained in the digital realm, monitoring the global networks that would now carry the hopes and dreams of a community that had finally found its authentic voice.

"Eleanor would be proud," Lucas said, his prophetic senses showing him visions of a future where supernatural abilities were integrated into human civilization as forces for healing, protection, and progress rather than domination or destruction.

"Eleanor would be amazed," Maya replied, her technopathy touching the edges of possibilities that expanded beyond anything the medieval visionary could have imagined. "She saw the problem clearly, but the solution required tools that wouldn't exist for six hundred years."

Outside the virtual space, the world continued its ancient rhythms, but now with the knowledge that some of its inhabitants possessed abilities that transcended ordinary human limitations. In hospitals, gifted healers worked openly alongside conventional medical professionals. In research institutions, enhanced individuals contributed insights that accelerated scientific discovery. In schools, supernatural children learned to use their gifts responsibly while their ungifted classmates learned that human potential was more varied and wonderful than anyone had previously imagined.

The New Covenant had succeeded where Eleanor's original vision had failed, not by choosing between revelation and concealment, but by creating systems that made the choice unnecessary. The future was uncertain, as all futures must be, but for the first time in six centuries, it was a future that the supernatural community would face together, authentically, and with hope.

The age of secrets was ending. The age of synthesis had begun.

EPILOGUE - THE OPEN SECRET

Geneva, Switzerland

September 21, 2030

Maya Chen stood at the podium of the United Nations Assembly Hall, addressing representatives from 193 nations in her role as Director-General of the Global Supernatural Affairs Council. Five years after the end of the covenant's era of secrecy, the world had adapted to the reality of enhanced human capabilities with a pragmatism that would have amazed Eleanor Blackthorne—and probably disappointed those who had predicted either utopia or apocalypse.

"The annual report shows continued integration success across all measured parameters," Maya announced, her technopathy simultaneously translating her words into sixty-three languages while monitoring the emotional responses of delegates through their personal devices. "Supernatural contributions to healthcare have reduced treatment costs by an average of 12% across participating nations. Enhanced individual involvement in disaster response has decreased casualty rates by 34% compared to pre-integration baselines. Academic collaboration between gifted researchers and traditional institutions has accelerated technological development in renewable energy, communications, and medical technology."

Maya paused, allowing her words to settle across an audience that included both ordinary humans and openly supernatural individuals serving as diplomatic representatives. The integration hadn't been seamless—five years of adaptation had included policy disputes, regulatory challenges, and occasional conflicts between enhanced and unenhanced populations. But the catastrophic outcomes that had haunted Eleanor's visions for six centuries had failed to materialize.

"The key to our success," Maya continued, "has been the principle of managed transparency that allows supernatural abilities to contribute to human welfare while protecting individual autonomy and preventing the concentration of enhanced power in any single institution or organization."

In the observer gallery, thirteen-year-old Sofia Vasquez watched with the careful attention of someone whose childhood manifestation had triggered the events that led to this moment. Now attending the International School of Geneva as part of the first generation of openly gifted students, Sofia represented something unprecedented in human history: a supernatural individual who had never needed to hide her true nature.

"The old fears were based on false assumptions," Sofia would later tell her classmates in an essay that would be published in Time magazine's annual "Voices of the Future" issue. "People thought that knowing about supernatural abilities would make ordinary humans feel inferior or frightened. Instead, it made them feel like human potential was more amazing than anyone had imagined."

Behind Maya on the Assembly Hall stage, Lucas Blackthorne served as Deputy Director for Prophetic Analysis, his role officially recognized by the international community that had learned to value accurate prediction of global trends and potential crisis points. His prophetic abilities were no longer hidden gifts that isolated him from normal human relationships, but professional qualifications that enabled him to serve humanity in ways that honored both his heritage and his individual talents.

"The global supernatural population is estimated at approximately 50,000 individuals with active abilities," Lucas reported during his portion of the address. "An additional 200,000 people carry dormant genetic markers that may manifest under specific circumstances. These numbers represent less than 0.01% of the human population, but their contributions to human welfare have been disproportionately significant."

Maya smiled as she felt the pride radiating from the assembled supernatural delegates. The community that had once hidden in basements and safe houses now included Nobel Prize winners, Olympic athletes whose abilities were officially acknowledged and regulated, CEOs of companies that had revolutionized their industries through enhanced human capabilities, and government officials who served openly while managing supernatural gifts that made them uniquely qualified for their roles.

The transformation hadn't eliminated all challenges. International law still struggled with questions about the rights and responsibilities of enhanced individuals. Some religious communities continued to debate the theological implications of supernatural abilities. Economic systems were adapting to contributions that couldn't be easily quantified or replicated through normal human labor.

But these were the ordinary difficulties of social evolution rather than the existential threats that Eleanor had foreseen in her medieval visions.

Boston, Massachusetts

Same day

In a classroom at the Eleanor Blackthorne Institute for Supernatural Studies—established in a renovated church that had once housed one of the covenant's oldest safe houses—Lucas spent his afternoons teaching the responsible use of prophetic abilities to young people who would never face the choice between authenticity and survival that had defined every previous generation of the gifted.

"Prophecy is not about predicting fixed futures," Lucas explained to his class of twelve students ranging in age from fifteen to twenty-two. "It's about perceiving the patterns that shape possibilities, then using that knowledge to guide choices that create better outcomes for everyone."

His students included Maria Santos from São Paulo, whose visions focused on environmental changes that could prevent ecological disasters; Jin Park from Seoul, who specialized in technological trends that informed international development policies; and Alex Thompson from Toronto, whose prophetic insights into social

309

movements helped organizations plan for peaceful transitions during periods of political change.

None of them would spend their lives hiding their gifts or serving organizations that demanded secrecy in exchange for belonging. They would graduate from the Institute to join the global community of supernatural professionals who worked openly within human institutions while maintaining connections to the enhanced community that provided mutual support and guidance.

"The most important lesson Eleanor Blackthorne learned," Lucas told his students as the afternoon class concluded, "is that gifts are meant to be shared, not hoarded. The tragedy of the old covenant wasn't that it demanded secrecy—it was that secrecy prevented the gifted from serving their full potential as contributors to human flourishing."

Phoenix, Arizona

Same evening

Elena Vasquez sat in her living room, reading news reports about Maya's UN address while Sofia worked on homework assignments that included both ordinary mathematics and specialized training in the responsible use of telekinetic abilities. The domestic tranquility of their evening represented something that would have seemed impossible five years earlier: a supernatural family living normal lives while fully authentic about their nature.

"Mom," Sofia said, looking up from textbooks that included both standard biology and advanced courses in supernatural physiology, "do you think great-great-grandmother would have approved of how things turned out?"

Elena considered the question while thinking about her own grandmother's stories of supernatural ancestors who had hidden their healing abilities even while working as midwives and folk healers in rural Mexico. The courage required to conceal power was different from the courage required to use it responsibly, but both forms of courage honored the same fundamental commitment to protecting vulnerable people.

"I think she would have been proud that you never had to choose between being yourself and keeping others safe," Elena replied. "That was always what she wanted—for our gifts to serve life rather than requiring us to live as shadows."

Outside their window, Phoenix had rebuilt itself as one of the world's first "integrated cities," where supernatural abilities were incorporated into urban planning and disaster preparedness. Sofia's middle school included both enhanced and unenhanced students working together on projects that combined ordinary human creativity with supernatural capabilities. The result was an educational environment that encouraged all students to explore the full range of human potential while learning to cooperate across differences that went far beyond the traditional categories of race, religion, or nationality.

Virtual Assembly Space

Global Network

In the digital realm that had become the primary meeting space for the global supernatural community, representatives from the network that had replaced Eleanor's covenant gathered for their monthly coordination session. The virtual environment had evolved far beyond Maya's original design, incorporating contributions from technopaths around the world to create spaces that existed simultaneously in multiple dimensions of reality.

"Integration challenges remain minimal across all regions," reported Dr. Sarah Chen from Vancouver, whose research into supernatural neurology had become foundational to the medical protocols that governed enhanced individual healthcare. "Public acceptance polling continues to show approval ratings above 70% in countries with established integration programs."

"Economic impact assessment shows net positive contributions in all measured sectors," added Carlos Mendoza from São Paulo, whose abilities had evolved from street art to large-scale environmental restoration projects that were helping to reverse climate change damage across South America.

"The old covenant remnants continue to diminish," noted Agent Patricia Williams, whose role had evolved from federal law enforcement to international liaison for supernatural affairs. "Fewer than 200 individuals worldwide maintain traditional concealment

312

practices, and most of those are elderly community members who prefer privacy rather than active opposition to integration."

Maya listened to the reports with satisfaction that was tempered by awareness of ongoing challenges. The supernatural community had avoided Eleanor's catastrophic futures, but they had also assumed responsibilities that would define human civilization for generations to come. Enhanced individuals were no longer isolated by secrecy, but they were also no longer protected by invisibility. Their successes and failures would be judged by standards that applied to any group with disproportionate influence on global affairs.

"The work continues," Maya announced as the session concluded. "We've ended the cycle of secrecy that defined our past. Now we build the cycle of service that will define our future."

Eleanor's Grave

Blackthorne Family Cemetery, Connecticut

Lucas stood beside the simple stone marker that bore his ancestor's name, carrying flowers and the final pages of Eleanor's hidden journal—the passages that had been sealed even from him until the New Covenant's establishment had proven that her deepest hopes had finally been realized.

"If future generations read these words," Eleanor had written in her final entry, "it means that the choice I feared has been transcended through wisdom I could not possess. The gifts we carry were never

313

meant to divide us from humanity, but to connect us more deeply to the sacred responsibility of serving life in all its forms.

"I have seen darkness and called it inevitable, but perhaps inevitability is simply the failure of imagination. Perhaps the future can be brighter than any past, more inclusive than any tradition, more hopeful than any fear.

"Let my descendants know that their ancestor's greatest vision was not of catastrophe prevented, but of gifts finally freed to serve their true purpose: the healing of the world."

Lucas placed the flowers on Eleanor's grave and spoke words that would have seemed impossible during six centuries of supernatural secrecy: "The mission is complete. The gifts are free. The healing has begun."

As he walked away from the cemetery that held the remains of twenty-seven generations of his family, Lucas felt the weight of inherited obligation finally lifting from his shoulders. The prophetic burden that had defined the Blackthorne bloodline for six centuries had been transformed into something lighter and more hopeful: the gift of seeing possibilities rather than inevitabilities, the joy of guiding choices rather than preventing disasters.

The age of secrets was over. The age of service had begun.

And in schools and hospitals, laboratories and disaster zones, corporate boardrooms and refugee camps around the world, supernatural individuals worked openly alongside their unenhanced neighbors to build a future that honored both human limitations and human transcendence, both individual authenticity and collective responsibility.

Eleanor Blackthorne's vision had been fulfilled, not through the prevention of catastrophe, but through the creation of possibilities that made catastrophe unnecessary. The choice between revelation and concealment had been replaced by the ongoing choice between fear and hope, between isolation and community, between gifts hoarded in darkness and gifts shared in light.

The open secret was no longer that some humans possessed supernatural abilities.

The open secret was that all humans possessed the capacity for growth, for adaptation, for building worlds that honored both what they were and what they could become.

The story that had begun with a young woman's terrifying vision in a plague-ravaged village ended with a global community that had learned to see possibilities rather than inevitabilities, to choose hope rather than fear, to serve the future rather than remain imprisoned by the past.

The cycle was complete. The new cycle had begun.

And somewhere in the quantum foam of possibility that surrounded all human choices, Eleanor Blackthorne's spirit rested in peace, knowing that her people had finally found their way home.